# Indebted To The Vampires

Lilly Wilder

Published by Lilly Wilder, 2022.

This is a work of fiction. Similarities to real people, places, or events are entirely coincidental.

INDEBTED TO THE VAMPIRES

**First edition. November 24, 2022.**



ISBN: 979-8223837053

Written by Lilly Wilder.

# Table of Contents

# Indebted To The Vampires

**By: Lilly Wilder**

# Foreword

My name is Elsa Carpenter and if you were to look at me you'd think I'm just an ordinary 18 year old girl, but I'm not. I'm a Slayer with an ancient duty to fight against evil. It turns out vampires were the least of things I had to deal with. Upon my acceptance into the prestigious Angel Academy, I crossed the strict headmaster, who was always on my case and this bled over to some...disagreements with my peers. I started to get bullied. Can you believe that? A Slayer getting bullied by ordinary people! I couldn't use my Slayer skills. I had to be smarter.

Then, my world was thrown into even more disarray when I met three hot vampires who helped me out of a tight spot. I know I was meant to hate them, but loving them was so wrong, it felt so right.

# Indebted To The Vampires

# Chapter One

It was a dark street. The moon hung brightly in the sky, like a lantern. The stars glittered around them. The city was empty, dead. It was the time of night when most sane people were in bed with their loved ones, either sleeping or fucking. That was how normal people lived, but I wasn't normal. I clenched my jaw and continued walking. There was something in the air, something deadly. The rain had been falling all day, but now the sky was dry. I avoided stepping in puddles, not wanting to give away my position. This was the time of night when monsters came out to play, and my job was to put them down.

I peered into the shadows. That's where they liked to hide, vampires, the scourge of my existence. I remember clearly, the first day I'd learned of their existence, I mean their actual existence, not their place in the mythical pantheon of horror. There was truth to the story, more truth than people would like to admit. More truth than they could handle. I'd doubted myself, even when all the proof had been staring me in the face. It wasn't until I was standing there, pinning a vampire to the ground with a wooden stake, that I was a true believer, and I had to be, because I was a Slayer.

A long time ago, bloodlines had been blessed with strength and power. Those bloodlines had been nurtured and protected through the years. In every generation, one woman rose and embodied that strength and, this generation, it just happened to be me, little old Elsa Carpenter.

If you were to look at me you'd never think I was a monster hunter. I was about 5'4, petite, and I'd only just had my eighteenth birthday. I was struggling with trying to get into the prestigious Angel Academy where only the brightest minds were accepted, while at night I was hunting the creatures of the dark. I guess that was the trick of it, for us Slayers to hide in plain sight. I knew there were more like me out there but I wasn't allowed to know of their existence. Letting any vampires know our true nature was a Very Bad Thing, indeed, as I was told by my mentor, the ever reliable Arthur.

All I wanted was to be a normal girl but I wasn't allowed to be. Apparently my ancestors had made a pact that rippled out through the generations, until it touched me and forced me into a life I hadn't chosen, and I wasn't about to run from it now. I knew how dangerous vampires could be. I'd seen what they were capable of and if I can stop them, then I had to try, I just had to hope that I could balance my own life as well.

Movement in the shadows. I know he's there. I reach down and pull out the wooden stake, a trusty weapon. I crouch, using my heightened senses to try and pull away the veil of the night. An ordinary human wouldn't stand a chance and even though I have enhanced abilities the odds are still stacked against me. I hear a noise and shift to the left but no, it's a distraction. I notice too late.

To the right there's a screech and the pale face of a vampire leers at me. Its fangs are bared and its hands are outstretched, its spindly fingers tinted with sharp tips, ready to tear my supple flesh apart. My heart thunders inside but I keep my cool. I'm a Slayer. This is what I was born for. I twist back and evade its attack, arching my body, then bringing my legs up to kick it in its head. It rears back. My blow shocking him more than anything. It takes more than physical damage to bring these suckers down. I get into a defensive stance and watch the pale creature stare at me with its beady eyes. Its mottled skin shows that it has been starved of blood and is desperate. I can see the ravenous hunger, the rage. I lick my lips and keep my breathing steady. I know it's smelling my sweat, listening to my heartbeat, thinking how succulent it would be to sink its teeth into my flesh.

It should be taking more care. It should be more deliberate in its movements, but the hunger is driving it mad. The creature lashes forward, its mouth opened wide. I see the path it is taking. My instincts kick in and, at the last moment, I dive down and slide across the ground, sending up a splash of water as my feet hit a puddle. I thrust my arm up and slam the stake into its heart. There's a slight whimper, and then, I close my eyes as dust falls around me.

Once again, I'm disgusted by the ash that settles on my clothes, arms and hair. I do my best to not breathe it in. I've made that mistake already and the aftermath was not pleasant. I holster the stake and brush away the dirt, taking pride in another successful kill. I know they won't all be this easy. The city is teeming with these creatures. It's plagued with a mass of evil and I'm the cure, but for now they're going to get one more night of mercy because I have to sleep. I have an interview tomorrow to see if I'm accepted into the Angel Academy. God knows how I'm going to balance my studies with my extra-curricular activities but I'll find a way. I have to. I'm a Slayer.

I turn my back and walk through the empty streets. I look up at the houses and know that no one in them is ever going to thank me for keeping them safe. It is better they don't know, because then the whole world would go mad. I wonder how many vampires are out there now, watching me.

*

"How was your patrol tonight?" Arthur asked, when I returned home. Home was an old building that had been used by Slayers for generations. The organization was a global one, with operatives in many different countries and plenty of resources and assets. Investments had been made wisely over the years and once my powers developed I came to live with Arthur in our expansive townhouse. It was filled with all manner of artifacts and books. Arthur loved his books. He was a balding, round-shouldered man who had devoted his life to the study of vampires. We never had many guests, but we still tried to hide our specialized equipment just in case anyone ever came around. It was better to keep up appearances and hide our truth.

"It was standard," I said, grabbing a drink from the kitchen. "There were a few roaming about but I made sure they didn't get any victims.

"Good."

"Have you managed to track down any information about their nest, or who the local master is?" I asked.

"Unfortunately not, and it's proving to be quite vexing."

There was always a master, someone who was driving the vampires to achieve some agenda and who normally turned many of them to engender their loyalty to him. Occasionally, there were places where random vampires gathered and roamed about of their own accord. These were usually dealt with quite easily, but the infestation here, convinced us that the vampires were being led by a master, and a master who was likely in a high place in society. Some of the kills had been out in the open and there hadn't been a public panic yet. This meant that either the authorities were covering up the nature of the deaths for the sake of the people's sanity, or they were hiding the truth to protect their brood. I wasn't sure which one was more likely, but it sure made me suspicious.

"We'll get him," I said, confidently. Arthur gave me a weak smile. He evidently wasn't as convinced as I was.

"And how are you feeling about tomorrow?"

I shrugged and wiped some lingering orange juice from my lips. "I'm trying not to think too much about it. After all, it's not the end of the world," I joked.

"No, but you don't want it to be the end of your world. The Angel Academy will be good for you and open up many doors later on in your life. It will provide you many opportunities to progress."

"That's if the end doesn't happen before I get that old," I said dryly. That should be 'The End', with capital letters, an ancient prophetic warning that the undead would take this world in its grip and overwhelm humanity with an eternal curse. Some scholars dismissed it as ravings of an insane vampire who vastly overestimated the strength of his brethren, but some took it more seriously, especially vampires.

"You shouldn't talk about these things so lightly," he said.

"I know I've seen a lot of things that I never would have believed in had I not seen them with my own eyes, but I don't think words written hundreds of years ago have any bearing on what happens now. The Slayers have kept vampires in check so far and we'll keep on doing that. It's not like the line is going to be broken. Even if I die, someone else is going to take my place."

"Elsa, don't speak like that!" Arthur exclaimed, horrified.

I shot him a sideways glance. "Ever since I received this power, I've known my time is going to be short. What's the average life expectancy for a Slayer?" I asked.

Arthur licked his lips and his gaze darted to the floor.

"Exactly," I said, as he offered nothing in reply. "And I've made my peace with that. I'm going to try and enjoy myself for as long as I'm here, and I'm not going to try and think too far ahead. Because there might not be a far ahead."

My words were harsher than I intended them to be and I could see that Arthur was visibly hurt. I understood why. He had been my Aunt's handler, after all, the Slayer before me. But in truth I had been used to the idea of dying before my time, ever since I was young, in fact, since my parents had died in the car crash. They had been young too, and it seemed wrong that I should live past the point they did.

"I know that being a Slayer is a difficult task, and one that you didn't ask for, but that doesn't mean you have to be reckless. You can still have a long and happy life, if you put the work in. Elsa, I know you can succeed in whatever you do. Please, for my sake, try to get in to the academy. It will mean so much for your future prospects. This could be life-changing."

"As life-changing as being told that I have the power of a Slayer and that for generations my family has been fighting the undead forces of a vampiric army?"

"Perhaps not that life-changing," Arthur said, after a pause, "but unfortunately you need other talents to progress in the world, and it's healthy for you to form relationships outside of this circle. You shouldn't ever have to feel alone."

"Oh, how could I feel alone when I have you Arthur?" I replied somewhat flippantly. "I'm sure I'll be fine, I mean, who can resist my natural charm? You don't have anything to worry about. I'll kill the interview, just like I kill vampires."

I shot him a wink, although he still looked troubled and didn't seem comforted by my attitude at all, but Arthur was always cautious. I suppose I couldn't blame him, considering that he was just a mortal and felt vulnerable against vampires and, also, because of what happened to my aunt. I should have gone a little easier on him, considering that he was the only family I had, but he was such an easy man to tease because he took everything so seriously. I suppose it would be good to at least broaden my social horizons and have some friends my own age, although making friends had never been something I was particularly good at.

*

I retreated upstairs to my room and put aside my weapons, placing them back into the drawers where most girls my age would keep make up and pretty jewelry. Instead of those trinkets I had a silver dagger, stakes, and a vial of holy water. I gazed out of my window at the starry sky and the silver moon, and I wondered how many vampires were still roaming around unchecked. It was impossible to tell exact numbers, since only Arthur and I were working the area, and I wasn't about to go and try to take a head count. However, I encountered some every night, and I was slowly working my way through the trickle of them, trying to find where they were all spawning from. My work as a Slayer was never done, and somehow the interview with the Angel Academy paled in comparison, when I thought about the importance of the two. But, then again, it wasn't as though the wider world would ever know of my efforts as the Slayer.

I was reminded of that old philosophical thought about a tree falling in a wood making no sound, and I found a similarity in my own situation. If the rest of the world never knew about my exploits did they really matter? I think that's why Arthur was so insistent on me attending the academy; so that I had something other than slaying vampires to fill my days and nights. Saving the world could easily become an obsession, but it wasn't as though there was an end in sight. Vampires were present all over the world and us Slayers, were spread out far and wide, so we could never commit to an all-out assault. All we could do was manage their population and limit the damage they could do. We were caught in a balancing act.

I knew there was another reason why Arthur wanted me to cultivate a life in the outside world, although we didn't talk about it. You see, the Slayer ability was passed down through the bloodlines, so the only way to truly kill a Slayer is to kill the last woman in her bloodline. Currently, that's me. I have no sister and my aunt never had children. She died before she could have a family and I knew that, for the good of the world, I should have a daughter of my own to ensure that there was a warrior to take my place one day, but that was almost too much to ask.

Going out every night to kill vampires? Sure thing, I can do that, but having a family? That means falling in love, forming attachments, making myself vulnerable...I wasn't sure about that. Physical pain could heal, but emotional pain, that was the one that really scarred.

It wasn't as though I'd ever been taught how to be a parent either. My parents had died when I was very young, so young that I barely remember them now. Their faces are ghosts in my mind and their voices are just whispered echoes. I still have a scar on my stomach from the car crash. Sometimes it haunts my nightmares as well.

I was taken to an orphanage, being told that I had no family who wanted to claim me. I learned how to survive, how to fight for what I wanted, but no family ever wanted me. Maybe they sensed I was different. Maybe they saw something in my eyes but, whatever it was, they left me to rot in that place. I was unwanted and that was the most painful thing of all.

The nuns who ran the orphanage made sure I had a good education, but it didn't seem like my prospects were going to be any good in the real world.

Then Arthur had come along. I'll always remember that day. I was helping to teach one of the younger girls to read, and I had been filled with such pity, and even a little bit of envy. I'd seen so many kids come and go from the orphanage. There were only a few who were like me, and nobody could explain why, it was just one of those unfortunate things that happened. I knew that this other girl was going to be chosen and given a loving home, provided with love, care, support, and all the things that a kid should have, but I was never going to have that. My childhood had disappeared and it could never be claimed back. It was just gone, vanished, and I would always mourn the childhood I could have had.

But I was teaching her to read, and then, Sister Agatha came to me with a strange look on her face. She said there was someone I needed to meet. Arthur was standing there with his briefcase in hand, wearing his brown suit that was a little too tight for him. He smiled at me weakly.

"Elsa," he said, "I have to speak with you. I knew your aunt."

My first reaction had been one of anger.

"If I had an aunt then why didn't she get me out of here?" I screamed.

Arthur went on to explain that she had a dangerous line of work and she didn't want to put me in danger, but that she had died. As if it wasn't bad enough that I learned I had an aunt who didn't want anything to do with me, now I learned I'd just lost the last family I had. Arthur handed me a letter from her and told me to read it.

I couldn't believe what I was reading. She talked about the bloodline and tried to explain her actions and why she had stayed away. She also talked about my parents and had a few trinkets of theirs. It was nice to read about her memories of them, and I still wear a pendant that was my mother's even today. I looked at Arthur with disbelief when I read the part about the Slayers.

"You have to be kidding me," I said.

Arthur glanced around and lowered his voice to a conspiratorial whisper.

"It's all real. You're going to start to feel different soon. I know you don't believe me, but when you do, come to this address." He handed me a card with an address stamped on it. He left my aunt's possessions with me and then he departed. I thought he was a kooky old man and I had no idea what had happened to my aunt, but it seemed she had lost her mind. I didn't think anything of it at the time, but later that night and through the next few days I did feel different. I felt stronger and faster, and I wasn't sure what was happening. I was beginning to have dreams, as well, but they didn't feel like my dreams, they were the dreams of other people from long ago, people I didn't even know.

Eventually, I went to Arthur and he told me everything. The dreams turned out to be echoes of my ancestors, and he assured me they would calm as I became used to my new powers. I still wasn't sure if this was all real, or if it was some kind of elaborate magic trick, but then he asked me if I would rather live in denial and go back to the orphanage, living an ordinary life, or take a chance, believe him, and become something greater than I ever could have imagined.

I chose the latter, obviously, and I didn't regret my choice. My life was firmly divided into two parts and, at least, being a Slayer I knew I had my place in the world. But that wasn't enough. I had to go out there and be something else as well. I pulled the covers tightly around me and welcomed the few hours of sleep I was going to get, because the interview for the academy beckoned and despite my show of bravado and nonchalance in front of Arthur, I was nervous.

# Chapter Two

I was in a dark castle. Wings of bats fluttered behind me. I gasped, looking at the grey stone. I was on an altar, wearing a dark robe. It was so cold. The stone was hard. Shadows danced around the room. My skin was pale. Three figures emerged from the darkness and immediately, I knew them to be vampires. They smiled, showing their fangs. I gasped. My heart fluttered with terror and I tried to push myself away, tried to escape. I reached for my stake, but my arms wouldn't move. My body wouldn't do as I commanded.

This wasn't a dream. This was a memory, an echo of one of my ancestors. I winced in terror as it was likely the time she died. The three vampires came closer. I knew I was going to have to feel their fangs sinking into my flesh. I tried to scream in terror. Why wasn't the Slayer moving? Why wasn't she struggling to flee? Why wasn't she screaming?

The vampires were mere inches away. I knew the final moment was approaching so I braced myself. But then, to my shock, the vampires fell to their knees and bowed to me.

"Mistress," they said, and then the dream faded...

*

"Did you sleep well?" Arthur asked when I came downstairs. The dawn sun was bright, twinkling against the morning dew that trickled down the windows. Birds chirped outside and on a morning like this it was difficult to believe that monsters existed in the world.

"Like a baby," I said. "No nightmares at all," I lied. I wasn't yet sure what that dream meant. I was convinced that it was an echo of a memory, rather than a dream, because I had become adept at telling the two apart, but I was confused by the content. I'd never experienced anything where vampires bowed to me. It didn't fit with anything, and

I wasn't ready to share it with Arthur just yet. I wanted to think on it myself first.

Some nights were good and some were bad. This one, I wasn't even sure how to classify. It was just new.

The kitchen smelled like bacon and eggs. Arthur brought out a stacked plate.

"You'll need your strength today. I don't want you going into that interview on an empty stomach," he said. I gulped down some orange juice and thanked him, before tucking heartily into my breakfast. Arthur was a man of many talents and cooking was but one string to his bow. Everything was perfect. "How are you feeling?"

"Fine, I'll admit, now that it's getting closer I am feeling a little nervous, but I'm sure I'll be okay."

"I'm sure you will too. Just remember to answer their questions honestly, although don't be afraid to embellish a little. Present the best version of yourself to them and I'm sure you'll be fine. In many ways, this interview is just a formality. I think they just want to meet you and ensure that you're the type of person who will fit in at the academy."

"I'll be my normal charming self," I flashed him a smile.

"Indeed," Arthur replied.

"And what are you going to do while I'm at the interview?" I asked.

"I requested some new tomes to be delivered and they just arrived at the library, so I think I shall peruse them."

I couldn't stop thinking about the dream, so I did venture to ask Arthur one question.

"Arthur, what would happen if a Slayer became a vampire?"

Arthur's face paled. "That would be a very bad thing indeed, and it's not something we like to think about."

"Has it ever happened?"

"No, and it's my job to ensure that it never will. Don't think of such matters, it will only lead you down a dark path of doubt and fear."

His answer troubled me, not just the content of it, but the way the words were rushed. Arthur was usually a placid man and it took a great deal to rouse passion within him, so there definitely seemed to be more to this. It was the first time that I really doubted him. There was so much I didn't know about Arthur and the history of Slayers as a whole. Everything had I learned had been from Arthur, and I thought I should do some research of my own because I felt something from that dream, something dark and powerful, and it wasn't as easy to dismiss as Arthur seemed to think.

Becoming a vampire had only been something I thought about in passing. I was confident in my abilities as a Slayer, but not to the point where I was reckless. Arthur had warned me that a Slayer's greatest downfall was her own ego, and I had assumed he was talking from experience regarding what had happened with my aunt. I had asked him how she died, but it evidently caused him great pain. The two of them had been close for a long time and he wasn't just her mentor; he was her friend. He said she had made a mistake that had cost her everything, and since he pushed me so hard to concentrate and be mindful of my surroundings, I could only assume that she had let her guard slip in battle and a vampire she fought was able to kill her.

So far, none of the vampires I had faced had been deadly or skilled. The ancient ones were the ones Slayers had to worry about. The only danger from the minions was their number, for as powerful as she was, she was just one warrior against an army.

However, for the time being, I had to push those worries aside and focus on my interview. After breakfast I got dressed and then Arthur was ready with the car to drive me to Angel Academy. I watched the world whiz by as we circled the city and made our way to the large academy that was situated in the woods. It was a private, prestigious place that offered students a varied education. Ordinarily, I wouldn't have been able to get in, but the Slayer organization had garnered a lot of favors over the years and one of them had been influence in the academy. It also helped that a sizeable donation had been made recently. I wasn't a fan of how the world worked but it seemed logical to take advantage of it.

The road turned into an avenue that was lined with trees. Their leaves were lush and the trunks were wide and sturdy. They were so tall it seemed as though they were standing guard. The avenue was straight and it led up to black iron gates tipped with gold. A stone wall ran around the perimeter and a plaque had been nailed into the pillar. There was a buzzer next to the gate and a place to swipe a card. Since we didn't have a card, Arthur pressed the buzzer and announced our arrival. The gates swung open slowly, creaking. The tires of the car crunched the gravel of the drive. It was straight and the lawn stretched out for acres.

The gravel drive led up to a fountain and the gravel path formed a circle around this centerpiece. I gazed in awe at the fountain. It was a grand design that stood about six feet tall by my estimation. Cherubs sat around the rim of the lowest bowl of the fountain, and in the middle an angel rose up high, its wings and arms spread out, and its neck was arched back as it gazed up to heaven. Cherubs clung to this angel, and around the angel were shells, harps and trumpets. Water trickled down over its wings and into the main fountain. It was a resplendent sight, and the pose was so dynamic, I almost expected the angel to ascend and soar through the sky.

The main building stood before us, tall, wide and imposing. The red bricks were bright and the sun gleamed on the wide windows, making it look as though they were winking as we drove up.

Arthur parked the car and opened the door for me. He checked that I had everything I needed and then he wished me luck.

"I'll return in a few hours," he said. I nodded and watched him depart. The car traveled back up the gravel path and receded into the distance. I turned, took a deep breath, and made my way up the stairs to the large doors. As I grew closer I heard the sounds of people moving around, and as I looked up, I wondered how many students came here. I wore a blouse and trousers, which were about the smartest things I owned, and I carried with me all the documents from the orphanage, which showed my test results and academic ability.

Arthur said this interview was merely a formality, but I wasn't sure I believed him. I wasn't even sure that I would fit in here, but he was convinced that it would be a good place for me, and I was willing to endure a few years of hardship if it meant I could have some better opportunities in life afterwards. I never wanted to be dependent on anyone and I never wanted to feel as helpless as I had done in the orphanage. I wanted control over my own life in case I was ever abandoned again.

My boots clacked over the marble floor as I entered. There was a pattern etched into the floor and there were paintings hung all around the oval lobby. There were doors at regular intervals, leading to different parts of the academy, and a staircase that rose to another level. The doors were open and more sound poured through, the sound of life, and yet I felt so distant from them while standing out here. There were portraits hanging on the walls, of academics who were held in high esteem. The biggest and most prominent was of William Angel, the founder of the academy.

I walked up to the reception desk and mentioned that I was there for an interview. She smiled at me, checked a book, and then had me sign in. She gave me a visitor's badge and instructed me to wait for someone to call me. I perched on a wooden bench and took in more of my surroundings. It was such a pristine place; it seemed a world away from the orphanage in which I had grown up. I gazed at the portraits of all the academics and it seemed as though they were staring back at me. I wondered if any of them had ever known the truth about the world. This seemed to be a place that was untouched by evil, and it was easy to forget that out there, in the nearby city, undead monsters roamed freely.

In here, I was just a normal girl with everything to prove.

"Miss Carpenter? If you'd like to come this way," a voice said. I looked up as my name was uttered and saw a prim lady opening a door for me. She wore a green shirt, and a pleasing smile. Perhaps it wouldn't be as bad as I thought. She led me through a narrow corridor into a room where two other people were sitting. She gestured for me to take a seat, and then introduced herself and the others.

"I'm Mrs. Thorpe, this is Headmaster Griff and the Head of Academics Mr. Hanon."

They nodded in turn. My gaze drifted to all three of them. The two men were slim and pale, with high cheekbones and grey eyes. The Headmaster, especially, seemed to glower and I only felt comforted by Mrs. Thorpe.

"Thank you for seeing me, it's an honor to be here," I said, trying to remember to be polite and respectful. I placed my file on the oak table but none of them seemed concerned with it. The walls were adorned with leather bound books and they each had a notebook in front of them, with a pen, although none of them had taken the pen in their fingers.

"I see that you have received no formal education," Headmaster Griff said. I was taken aback by how harsh he was. It didn't seem like an accommodating question and it took me a few moments to compose a response.

"While I didn't attend a high school, I did receive an education from the nuns that ran the orphanage. As you see here," I pushed the file a little nearer to him, although the Headmaster made no move to take it, "I have proven myself academically."

"You were raised in an orphanage; that must have been very tough. Can you tell us a little bit about that?" Mrs. Thorpe asked.

"Well, I was there from a young age, as my parents died in a car crash. I learned to fend for myself. The nuns were incredible and took great care of me, and they taught me as much as they could. As I grew older I took on more responsibility, and helped them run the orphanage, and teach the younger children. I think this is a good example of my initiative and proof that I was able to grasp knowledge enough to teach it to others," I replied, smiling proudly, as I thought I had given a very good answer.

"Why were you never adopted?" Headmaster Griff asked. My brow furrowed and my mouth dropped open. I couldn't believe he had asked me such a thing. Mrs. Thorpe seemed shocked, as well, but she didn't say anything. Mr. Hanon was unmoved.

"I...it was just one of those things I suppose. I don't think there is a single reason for it," I said.

"Are you a troublemaker? We have no need for troublemakers here," the headmaster asked.

"No, in fact, as I said, if you look in this file there are reports from the nuns and they have all given me glowing reports."

"Why did you apply to Angel Academy?" Mr. Hanon asked. I was relieved to be given a respite from Headmaster Griff's interrogation.

"I'd like to better myself and make up for some of the lack of formal education in my life so far. I am tenacious and determined, and I want to make something of my life. I want to look back and know that I gave myself every chance to succeed. I want to learn and discover my passions in life. I want to cultivate a good understanding of all the important areas of the world and leave it a better place than when I entered. I also want to show other people in my position that anything is possible, that even if you feel like you have nothing, as long as you have a determination to succeed you can achieve anything you want in life. There were times when I used to feel that life was hopeless."

The more I spoke, the more I realized how much I wanted to be at this academy for my own good, rather than just because Arthur suggested I go here. I realized that I had done little with my life and I did want to show other orphans that they could accomplish something. It suddenly all took on a new tension, as I realized that there was a chance I could fail. The headmaster had clearly taken a dislike to me for whatever reason; perhaps I wasn't the right fit for the image of the academy, so I knew I had my work cut out for me to convince them all that I could be welcome here.

"You know, it was heartbreaking to see people come in to the orphanage and then to see them walk out again, to know that I wasn't good enough, even though I hadn't done anything wrong. I had no idea why people left without me and there were points where I thought it was going to destroy me from the inside out. I thought I would never have any worth in life and there was no point to me doing anything. The nuns helped show me that I could be someone. That no matter what, I always had myself and my own ambition, and the most important thing was to prove these people wrong, to show them that I did have worth and that they had made a mistake by not taking me. I changed my way of thinking and I poured myself into my studies. This academy is designed to help people like me have the best chance of a good life, and that's all I'm asking for, a chance. I want to be better than I am."

It was Mr. Hanon, who, eventually, leaned over and picked up my file. He perused it while Mrs. Thorpe made some notes. Headmaster Griff remained unmoved. My gaze darted up, but I averted it immediately as he stared at me. He seemed to be transfixed on me and I had no idea why.

"Do you think you'll be able to meet the high standards we set here at the Angel Academy?" Headmaster Griff asked. "We only want the best of the best and we have a very rigorous code of behavior. Anyone in violation of this, is subject to termination, and anyone who doesn't apply themselves to their studies is subject to termination as well. Do you think you can give everything you have to this place? It will require all of your concentration. There can be no distractions."

I gulped and lied to him. "I promise I'll do everything I can to succeed here." It wasn't a promise I was going to be able to keep, because

I couldn't surrender my duties as a Slayer, but I wasn't going to blow this opportunity and I knew I'd be able to figure out a way to make this work.

"I think that's all we need to know for now. Why don't you step outside and we'll come and talk with you shortly, we just need a few moments to discuss a few things," Mrs. Thorpe said.

I nodded and thanked them for their time. I left the room and went back to the lobby. My knees quaked and my heart quivered. I returned to the safety of the bench and inhaled deeply, hoping that I had made a good enough impression, because I knew this place could really help me. I waited for about fifteen minutes, then Mrs. Thorpe came out, and by the smile that adorned her face I assumed it was good news, and indeed, she confirmed that I had been accepted.

"Thank you so much!" I said. "I was so afraid, especially after the headmaster seemed so...unimpressed with me."

"I wouldn't worry too much about him. He's always an inscrutable man." She lowered her voice. "He likes to put on an aura so that he can keep the students in line. I think it was more for effect than anything else."

I accepted her assessment of the situation but something still didn't sit right with the way he had acted around me. However, that was a problem for a later time. All that mattered was that I had been accepted.

Mrs. Thorpe offered to show me around, and since I still had a while to wait for Arthur to come and pick me up, I readily accepted her offer. She took me through one of the doors that led through a wide hallway with a varnished floor.

"I think most people are in class now," she said. Indeed, as we passed by the rooms I saw them filled with students. It felt strange to be in this kind of setting. The classes at the orphanage had always been small affairs and usually there was a constant rotation of faces as kids got adopted. "Do you know what you're going to study yet?"

"I haven't made my final choice; I didn't want to risk jinxing this interview, but I have made a shortlist, so when I get home I'll whittle it down. I definitely want to study history, and perhaps English Lit as well. I want to try and get as broad an education as possible so I can learn what really interests me."

"That's a good way to go about it. I think life is better when it's an adventure. I speak to some people here and they have everything planned out to the nth degree. They leave no room for anything unpredictable and life is always unpredictable."

"I agree," I said. Mrs. Thorpe seemed like a good sort and I was glad she was giving me this tour rather than either of the men. We didn't go into any of the classrooms, as we didn't want to disturb the classes that were in session.

"Are you going to live here?" she asked, resting a hand on a banister that led up a set of wide stairs.

"No, I'm going to commute. I live near here and, well, I couldn't afford the extra accommodation fees," I said. Mrs. Thorpe took her hand away from the banister.

"I suppose there's no need to show you the dormitories then," she said, chuckling to herself. The truth was that I would have liked to stay at the Academy, as it would have made things much easier for myself and Arthur, but it would have been almost impossible to keep up my extra-curricular nocturnal activities. The gates were such that it would have been difficult to creep outside, especially every night, and I didn't want to have to try and explain to people where I was going. I also didn't want to get a reputation of being truant. I didn't want to do anything to jeopardize my position here, as I got the feeling that the headmaster would be keeping a close eye on me.

"Now, this is what we're especially proud of," Mrs. Thorpe said, as she showed me to some huge double doors. She opened one of them and bright sunlight poured through a stained glass window, making colors dance across the floor. The hall was massive. There were two levels, and each one was crammed with books. There were tables where students sat, and shelves and shelves of books. "This is our pride and joy," she said. "There are some rare books here. It's a collection that has been curated over the generations and there's always something of interest to be found. I did once make it my mission to read every book in the library but I don't think I'll ever succeed."

"It's quite a daunting challenge," I said.

"Right now it's quite empty, because most students are in class, but when it comes to assignment time this place is filled and you might have to reserve a seat. There are smaller study areas situated throughout the academy as well, and there are some private rooms you can reserve. I don't want to stay here too long because I don't want to disturb those who are here."

I took a last, lingering gaze around and I caught a glimpse of three guys sitting at a table. Two of them had their backs to me but the one facing me smiled. I was caught off-guard because I was so used to going unnoticed but I offered a clumsy smile back. He was cute and going to this academy was quickly becoming quite a good idea after all.

Next, Mrs. Thorpe took me to the dining area and it was here where a disaster happened. We turned the corner and were so lost in conversation that we didn't look where we were going and clattered into a girl coming the other way. She was flanked by another girl and two boys, and as we collided, the tray she held flipped back and the food exploded over her clothes. The cloying sauce clung to her hair and splattered over her face, the meat hung on her body and left stains over her clothes. The drink she had cascaded over her and poured down her stomach and legs. She looked stunned, had been turned into a complete mess, and when she composed herself she looked at me with great ire.

"I'm so sorry," I said, holding up my hands. This girl narrowed her eyes at me, and if looks could kill, I would have been dead right there on the spot. She lowered her voice and her fists clenched by her side.

The color drained from her face, making her appear even paler than she already was. I'd learned a long time ago, even before I was a Slayer, to sense signs of aggression and she was visibly throbbing with anger.

"Who the hell are you?" she hissed. Then, her friend grabbed her arm and nodded towards Mrs. Thorpe. The pale, messy girl's gaze turned from me. For a moment it had seemed as though I was the only one who existed in her world and every part of her was focused on me but as soon as she saw Mrs. Thorpe her intensity softened.

"This is Elsa Carpenter. She's a new student here and I'm showing her around. Elsa, this is Julia, who I'm sure doesn't need reminding that we're always meant to be welcoming to new people."

"Welcome to Angel Academy," she said through gritted teeth. Then, a wicked smile appeared on her face. "I'm sure when you start your studies, I can show you around properly and let you know how this place works."

The threat in her voice was not thinly-veiled at all and I was annoyed that before I'd even started here properly I had already made an enemy. I wasn't averse to conflict, because in the orphanage we were all territorial, but at least there I had the superior footing, as I had been there for the longest time. Here, I was a stranger, a newcomer, and I didn't want to fall into the trap of being picked on. I apologized again in a conciliatory tone, as I and Mrs. Thorpe walked away. Julia continued gazing at me. I assumed she was plotting some way to get back at me for this accident.

"Julia is one of our brightest students. She can be difficult at times, but deep down she's a good person," Mrs. Thorpe said.

I wasn't sure I could trust her judgment in this matter. I was also worried about getting into direct conflict. I had the power to kill vampires. I wasn't supposed to use my gifts on mortals, and I remember now why I had always kept to myself. I hoped that not everyone in this place would turn out to be like her.

# Chapter Three

After showing me a few more rooms, Mrs. Thorpe took me outside and showed me the gardens. They were filled with all manner of floral species as well as interesting ornaments. Birds swooped down and landed on feeding bowls and there were a few people studying amid the sweet-smelling flowers. Beyond the garden was a thick forest and it looked an idyllic scene, like something out of paradise. The view had a calming sense and I knew I'd be spending a lot of time out here.

"I'm sure this is quite different from the city view you're used to," Mrs. Thorpe said.

"It is, indeed. It's so beautiful."

"Well, it's here to try and help remind people of the natural beauty of the world. The Angel family has always tried to cultivate a good sense of wellbeing and as the world has advanced they have tried to keep this place as basic and natural as possible. While we do encourage the use of technology to make studying easier, we also like them to take a look around at the world and not lose sight of what truly matters. We think it's all too easy to get caught up in the hectic pace of the world and one of our main principles, and one of the things we like to cultivate here, is a love of learning.

One of the things that stood out about your application, was that you were educated by nuns, rather than going through the public school system. We often find that people who have learned through less traditional means are more amenable to our methods and show a better passion for learning as an art in and of itself, rather than learning as a means to an end. We all want our students to better themselves, of course, but it pleased me to learn that you wanted to amass knowledge so you could help set an example for others in a similar position to yourself. Sadly, it seems that as time has marched on, some of the values we hold most dear have been left by the wayside. I'm sure someone as young as yourself wouldn't notice this sort of thing, but when you get to my age you start to see the dividing lines between the generations."

"I don't know, I've always thought I have something of an old soul. I think most people now, only want to learn information they think is relevant to them, rather than getting a well-rounded education. That's why places like these are so important. It's just a shame that they can't cater to everyone."

"No, well, if we did we'd only become like regular schools. We have to keep our student body selective so that we can maintain our standards. It's sad to admit," she sighed, "but we can't help everyone. Only those who want to help themselves."

"Well, I'm glad that you've decided you can help me," I said.

"Of course, I think you're going to be a very good addition to our academy. Now, when you get home, pick out the courses you want to study and we can arrange for you to join the classes. We don't keep to the traditional school year, so you can jump right in and if there's anything you don't understand I'm sure the tutors or your fellow students will be willing to help you."

I thanked her profusely for all her help and hoped that if I ever had to deal with the administrative side of the academy I could speak with her rather than the headmaster. She led me back to the lobby; thankfully I didn't have any more unfortunate encounters with other students and it wasn't too long before Arthur came to pick me up.

*

"Well, how did it go?" he asked, as we drove past the angel fountain and made our way home.

"It was just like you said, more of a formality than anything. I got in and all I need to do now is pick what I'm going to study. It seems like a good place, very peaceful, with a couple of exceptions."

"Exceptions?" he asked, arching an eyebrow. I told him about the bad vibes I got from the headmaster and about the incident with Julia.

"That is unfortunate, although I'm sure they're not as bad as they seem now. Headmasters in places like these are like absent gods. I'm sure you won't even have to interact with him, and as for this Julia, well, you're a resourceful young woman and I'm sure that you can handle her. I shouldn't think there will be too many challenges standing in your way. Just focus on your studies. When you leave, you won't ever have to face any of your fellow students again. Are you looking forward to it?"

"I am, actually. I like that the emphasis is on learning rather than getting good grades. You should have seen the library there; I think it would be a dream come true for you. Speaking of which, how were your books?"

"Oh yes, very enlightening. I managed to procure a very rare book filled with herbal remedies that was written centuries ago. It's so interesting to see the recipes and the drawings that were made by hand. I doubt it has much interest to anyone but me, but it was fascinating to read. I also have one book about owls, one about the flora found in the south of England, and a book about the art of forging weapons. There's so much knowledge in the world and it's so disappointing that I won't ever be able to know it all."

"No, but you know more than most people," I said.

"This is true," Arthur accepted. "As do you."

I gazed out of the window idly. "I wish my parents could see me now. Do you think they'd be proud of me?"

"I'm sure they would be."

"I wish I could speak with them one last time, just to ask them what they had in mind for my life. I wish I knew what they wanted me to be. Did Aunt Jess talk about any of that?"

"Unfortunately, not. She never spoke much about her family and I never asked. It wasn't really my role to get personally involved. I know that not being there for you did play on her mind. She grieved terribly for your parents. It pained her to not be able to share this life with them."

"I hate that I never even got to know her. I suppose that at least she had you with her. At least she didn't have to be alone."

Arthur's grip tightened on the wheel. "Yes, she did."

"Sorry. I know you don't like talking about that."

"No, and today should be a happy occasion. This is the first step of the rest of your life and you should be looking forward to it."

*

We returned home and before I went out on patrol that night I looked at the syllabus to see what lessons were available to me. I went with my instincts and picked History and English Literature, I also went for Philosophy as well as Botany, just to add something a little different. The fact that I didn't have to pick everything that went into a specific career was freeing. I liked that I could mix and match different things and pursue my own interests, and I wished every school could have been like this. I emailed them the list and then it was time for me to go out on patrol. I was eager to get back out there, as I wanted to confirm to myself that I could marry these two separate parts of my life. I also wanted some time to think about my dream, as well, for it still troubled me.

I had never heard of a Slayer becoming a vampire, or of vampires bowing down to her. If this had happened, I assumed the Slayer organization would have wanted to keep things quiet, which meant I was going to have to figure things out for myself. The first thing I had to do was to try and get access to Arthur's books, as the answers would surely be in there. He had many rare volumes that documented the history of the Slayers, and my family tree specifically, since that was the bloodline he was guardian of.

Speaking of dreams, the one surprising thing to me was that I had never had a flash of memory from my aunt. I really wanted one, as well, for I hoped that it would contain some small glimpse of my parents, but I couldn't force a memory to come to me. They were just swirling in my subconscious and it was by pure random chance that they appeared. They were better than having nightmares at least.

I stalked the night with my hooded robe cloaking my appearance. I had my weapons ready and I prowled the empty streets, focusing on the alleys and sidewalks that were prone to having vulnerable people walking by, unaware of the danger posed by the creatures of the night. I was certainly aware why my organization kept the existence of vampires a secret from the general population, but sometimes, I wondered if it would actually be better to let the truth out, as at least then people could defend themselves. But, the secret had been guarded for generations and we had to play our clandestine game.

I blended into the shadows, moving stealthily, keeping watch, ever vigilant. I spotted a few women walking alone and I tracked them in case they caught the attention of a vampire. If I could narrow down the instances of a vampire attack, then Arthur and I might be able to triangulate the location of the lair. I had never taken on an ancient vampire before but I was itching to. Arthur wasn't sure I was ready for that. He thought I needed more practice, but I knew I was ready. I could feel it in my blood.

*

A couple of hours passed; it had been a quiet night so far. No vampires had appeared and the only scream I'd heard had been the result of a stupid prank. I ended up drawing a dagger across the tip of my finger. A drop of blood bloomed and oozed out, trickling down until it splashed on the ground. I slunk back into the darkness and waited, letting my blood drip. It took a while but, eventually, I heard movement and the familiar hiss of a hungry vampire.

I emerged from the shadows, taking it by surprise. I thrust out my palm and hit it in the chest, before spinning around and kicking it in the head. It staggered back and I drew my stakes.

"Where's your master?" I asked. The monster glared at me with its beady eyes. It lifted its claws and hissed once again. This was one of the more primal vampires. The hungrier they got, the more primal they got, and the recent vampires I'd been hunting had been totally savage. With more blood they became more human, but also more difficult to track. If I wanted answers, then I was going to have to find one of these more cultured vampires and make them talk. I wasn't going to get anything out of this one, so as it came towards me, claws and fangs bared, I threw a dagger with all my might, hitting it straight in its withered old heart. It froze, paralyzed for a moment, and then it shuddered and turned to dust. It let out one last, agonizing hiss before it crumbled. I stepped into the pile of ash and picked up my stake, rubbing off the dust, and then I made my way back home.

*

When I returned home Arthur was sleeping. He didn't always stay up to welcome me, trusting in my ability to return home safely. He had left a lamp on in the lounge, to offer me some illumination, as I hydrated and fed myself after a night of patrolling. The Slayer abilities inside me gave me more stamina, so I needed less sleep than the average person. I was used to staying up at night anyway, as I had been plagued with insomnia for most of my life. I was looking forward to my first day at the academy, but I was also worried about the vampire in our midst. It was taking longer to find clues to the ancient one's whereabouts than I would have liked. As much as I enjoyed going out on patrol I didn't want to spend my Slaying days taking out minions and weak vampires, because they would always come like a relentless tide. I needed to take out the main threat before it could do too much damage.

Since there was nothing I could do at that moment in time, I decided to head to bed and try to get some sleep before the big first day at the academy, but as I walked upstairs I passed the door to Arthur's study. It was where he kept the majority of his books and was the font of all his wisdom. I thought there might be some kernel of information in there about my ancestors, and perhaps some clue about my mysterious dream. He didn't like me going in there without his permission; Arthur was a very private man and he was often fussy about his possessions, but what he didn't know wouldn't hurt him, I thought. I carefully opened the door, turning the handle gently. The hinges made a slight creak. I slipped into the opening and tiptoed across the floor, turning on a lamp. There were stacks of books all piled around in a haphazard manner and I shook my head at the mess. The room smelled of musty books, and on the desk was a plate with crumbs resting on it and a drop of jam, as red as blood.

I started flicking through the books, trying to find one that detailed my family tree, but as I was investigating the various piles he had left, I heard footsteps behind me. Arthur was standing in the doorway, wearing a loose robe.

"What are you doing in here?" he asked calmly, although there was a thread of tension underlying his calm tone.

"Sorry Arthur, I just came back from patrol and I wasn't quite ready to sleep yet. I thought I'd just do some light reading before bed."

"You know I don't like you coming in here without my supervision. These books are rare and valuable. I can't take the risk that you'll damage them."

"I would hope that you'd have more faith in me than that by now," I sighed. "I'm sorry, it won't happen again."

"What were you looking for anyway?"

"I just wanted to know more about my bloodline really. I thought that learning about the Slayers who came before me would help me learn about myself."

Arthur held the door open and looked at me with a studied gaze. I dipped my head and appeared conciliatory, although his insistence of controlling what information was given to me was starting to become suspicious. He exhaled deeply and hung his head.

"Elsa, we have known each other for a few years now and in that time I have gotten to know you quite well, better than you might think. I know when you are not being entirely honest with me. What are you hiding from me?"

I stroked my chin and ran my hands through my hair. It seemed as though there was no point keeping a secret from him, and really he was probably the only one who could help me.

"I had a strange dream. One of the memories from a Slayer bled through, but it wasn't like any that I had experienced before."

"Was it your aunt?" he asked, and there was urgency to his tone.

I shook my head. "It was from a long time ago. I had pale skin and I was in a stone building. It was cold and it was nighttime. I was surrounded by three vampires, but they...they didn't attack me. They bowed down to me, as though they were in thrall to me and I didn't feel afraid at all. Whoever that Slayer was, she wasn't in danger."

Arthur had a thoughtful look on his face. "And you're sure this was a memory echo and not a dream?"

"I'm sure. Do you know of any one of my ancestors who might have experienced something like this?"

"I'm afraid not, but if it was a long time ago it's always possible that some records have gotten lost over time. It is a curious thing. I have never heard of vampires being in thrall to a Slayer before. For now I don't think we should pay too much attention to this as it was a long time ago but, if it happens again, please let me know. I will consult the records just to check if there is any note of something like this happening. I suppose there have been tales of Slayers going errant through the years..."

"Errant? You mean like they ran away?"

"Precisely. Not everyone is suited to the task, unfortunately. The blessing that is passed down by blood doesn't change someone's ambitions, we can only hope that they have the character to take on the role of a Slayer."

"And if they don't?"

"Then other measures have to be taken. Now, get some rest and try not to think on this any longer." He came further into the room and ushered me out, almost pushing me towards my own room. I was left feeling unsatisfied with his answers, but there was little I could do about it. It didn't surprise me that some knowledge had slipped through the cracks and I found myself intrigued by the idea that some Slayers wouldn't want to be Slayers. I suppose not everyone had been in the same situation as I had been; where they had had nothing to lose. I wondered what would have happened had I had a stable life with other ambitions. Being a Slayer could have ruined all that, although I liked to think that I had enough presence of mind to put the fate of the world above my own desires.

I slipped into bed and wished again that I had the opportunity to speak to my Aunt. I would have loved to know what it had been like for her when she found out she had been blessed as a Slayer. I wondered if she had taken to it as readily as I had. For me, there was really no choice. I would have done almost anything else rather than stay in that orphanage much longer. I wish I had the opportunity to talk to other Slayers, as well, and find out how they had adjusted to the lifestyle. As much as I was grateful to Arthur for mentoring me and teaching me everything I needed to know, there was nothing that could compare to sharing knowledge with my peers. We were kept apart for our own safety, but I would have liked some leeway because I couldn't talk about this with anyone else. It was one part of the academy I dreaded; the feeling that I was going to have to keep a part of myself hidden. No matter what happened, I was going to have to lie to other people. It was a lie performed in the name of the greater good, but a lie nonetheless.

I didn't like thinking about what the organization would do to Slayer's who didn't take on the mantle. It wasn't like we could give up the power by choice. The only way for us to lose the power was to die. I supposed that the organization would just keep hounding people until they eventually gave in and realized that being a Slayer was their destiny. They had to have some measures in place after all, because not all Slayers could be active at once. It was quite possible that a child could be given the power of a Slayer if something unfortunate happened to their mother. I've always been afraid of that. I know that any child of mine is going to be thrust into this life, and for the sake of the salvation of the world I have to have a child eventually, but is it really responsible for me to bring a child into the world knowing they're going to have no choice but be turned into a weapon against evil?

I suddenly began to wonder if my mother had known the truth as well. It must have been a blessing for my Aunt to know that she didn't have to have her own daughter because I existed. Maybe it was easier for her to not meet me so she didn't have to face the fact that I was going to be condemned to this life. At least I had Arthur. I don't know what I would have done without him.

# Chapter Four

Upon my arrival at Angel Academy I hoped that I wouldn't inadvertently anger any of the other students like I had the previous day.

I walked into the main lobby and signed in. Mrs. Thorpe was there to greet me and welcome me. She made sure I had the welcome pack and a map, as well as all the pertinent safety information, although she assured me that was only for a rare worst case scenario. She had marked my classrooms on the map and then sent me into the wild academy by myself. Thankfully there was no sign at all of the headmaster and I privately hoped I would never have to bother seeing him again in such close proximity.

My first lesson was in history, so I made my way to the west wing of the building and passed through some winding hallways. The windows were big and let the sunlight pour in, although they never reached the middle of the hallway, leaving a path of shadows straight down the middle. I kept to this path, occasionally stretching out my hand to let the sunlight play on the back of my palm. I flexed my fingers and it looked as though they were dancing. Paintings of various people and landscapes hung on the wall and there were a few students relaxing. None of them paid me much attention, aside from when I noticed Julia and her cronies waiting at the end of the hall. One of her friends nudged her. She looked around to see me, and her face fell into a thunderous scowl.

I groaned inwardly and braced myself for an intense encounter. I kept my head low and hugged the map to my chest, angling my path to try and avoid the small group, but Julia intercepted me.

"Oh look, it's the new girl, what was your name again, Elsie?" Julia asked.

"Elsa," I corrected.

"I think I prefer Elsie. It occurs to me that we never met properly yesterday. I'm Julia, this is Angelica, and this is Tommy and Aaron." She gestured to her friends respectively. Julia's dark hair had a purple streak in it and she wore a lace choker around her neck. Angelica was the opposite, blonde and shapely with full lips as though she had stepped out of a 50s pin up calendar. Aaron was a slim, tawny-haired boy, with darting eyes and a square jaw. Tommy was taller, broader, and as I looked closer I saw that he was wearing eyeliner. They positioned themselves so that they were surrounding me, making it more difficult for me to escape.

"We'd love to show you around," Julia said. She moved quickly and went to grab the map from my hand, but my reflexes were quicker and I kept hold of the map. She tugged so hard though that the map ripped, and she looked annoyed that she hadn't been able to get it all. She looked at the fragment she had taken and nodded.

"I see you're a woman of culture," she said, "Well, you won't need this. It's easy to find your way around here, and we'll always be on hand to help. I like welcoming new students to the school, it's always good to get an injection of fresh meat." She stepped closer towards me, closing the distance between us. I could smell the light fragrance of her perfume. "I'm not going to forget what happened yesterday. You made a deadly mistake by humiliating me and I'm going to make this place hell for you. Do you understand? And nobody is going to do a damn thing about it because you're nothing around here. Nobody even knows you."

She lowered her voice, as she said that last sentence, and the words dripped with venom. She chuckled lightly after she finished speaking and my first instinct was to slam her against the wall and teach her that threatening me was a mistake she didn't want to make twice. But Arthur had made it clear that I had to hide my true nature no matter what, and I'd already been told about the strict code of conduct here at Angel Academy. If I fought her I knew that it would reflect badly on me, and it wasn't as though her friends would tell the truth about Julia's behavior. As much as I hated it, I had to rein in my natural inclinations and try to just grin and bear this treatment.

"It won't happen again," I said.

"We'll see," Julia replied. She let the map fragment flutter to the floor. "Be seeing you! Oh, and have fun in Professor Shackleton's class, he hates when his students are late." she called out as she walked away, turning her back on me. Her cronies laughed as well and I realized I had just made four enemies.

I checked the time and cursed. I ran down the hallway, my footsteps hammering on the floor. Julia and her friends had already turned into another room. As I ran I twisted my head from left to right, looking for the room I needed. The numbers were on small gold plaques that shone when the light hit them, and as I passed them they began to blur into each other. I began to worry that I was never going to find this damned classroom, but when I quickly checked the map I was relieved to learn that I was only a turn of the corner away, and as I entered I flung the door open breathlessly, only to find an entire silent classroom staring at me.

*

"May I help you?" Professor Shackleton asked, arching a bushy eyebrow in my direction. He had been in the middle of explaining something when I entered, and now the other thirteen or so people in the class looked at me as well. The door closed behind me and I froze entirely. I looked at him dumbfounded, utterly embarrassed that I had to announce my arrival to the class in this way.

"I'm sorry, I'm new here. Elsa Carpenter. I just started. It took me a little while to find the room, and my map got a little torn." I held up the torn map and shrugged apologetically.

"Welcome to Angel Academy," he sighed wearily. "Hopefully you will learn plenty of useful things here, like how to look after your things. I'll let you off this time, considering you're new, but for future reference I do not tolerate people being late. If you are going to be late, then I would rather you don't bother coming to my lesson at all. Now, take a seat. Hopefully this disruption won't have derailed my entire lesson."

He gestured to the tables that were laid out in a U-shape. All the other students had their notebooks out and were looking at the teacher eagerly. Professor Shackleton leaned against his desk. His arms were folded across his chest and he continued talking even though I hadn't taken my seat yet. I scanned the faces of my classmate, they were all strangers save one; sitting at a corner was the boy from the library who had smiled to me. I felt a flush prickle my cheeks as I took a seat next to him. He gave a me comforting look as if to say 'we've all been there', although he dared not speak in case he would draw Professor Shackleton's wrath.

*

Once I had settled in I found myself enjoying the lesson. Professor Shackleton didn't hide any gruesome or grisly truths from the historical world and I learned plenty of interesting facts over the course of the lesson, and my appetite was whetted for more. Thankfully I didn't make any other errors during class, and I even managed to contribute to a discussion, which I hoped would improve my standing in Professor Shackleton's eyes. As we were packing up, the boy spoke to me.

"I wouldn't worry about it too much, he's like that with all the new students. I'm Josh by the way.

" Elsa," I nodded.

"I saw you in the library yesterday, right?"

"Yeah, that was me. I just got accepted. Things move pretty quickly around here."

"They don't like to waste time," Josh chuckled. "Have you got your dorm sorted out yet?"

"I'm not actually staying here. I live near the city."

"Oh, okay. How are you finding the academy so far?" We gathered our belongings and left the group. Other people fell into conversation with each other and left in their social groups. I was glad that Josh had started a conversation with me as I didn't want to feel like a lost little girl all over again.

"It's big, and I think it's going to take some getting used to, but I like the feel of it so far. I'm looking forward to learning and improving myself so we'll see how it goes. I have already made an enemy though."

"Oh really? That's impressive. I'd love to know who, unless it's me I mean, I don't think I've done anything to piss you off so far but I've been known to be mistaken before." He held his hands up and I found his easy humor pleasing.

"No, it's not you. You're safe...for now," I said, laughing myself. "It's a girl named Julia?"

"Ah yes, Julia," Josh said knowingly. He had soft blonde hair and carried himself with easy confidence, as though he knew who he was and what he wanted from life. He was around six feet, so I had to crane my neck up to look at him, and his eyes were blue. His skin was pale, and from the way most people looked around here it seemed they were all focused on their studies, as only a few of them looked as though they got any sun.

"You know her?"

"Everyone around here knows Julia. She likes to think of herself as the Queen Bee, which is why she surrounds herself with her friends and she knows how to wrap the faculty around her little finger, which is why she's confident at getting away with so much. How did you manage to get her attention so quickly? It usually takes at least a few weeks for people to get on her radar."

"I was walking into the dining hall and I wasn't looking where I was going, so I crashed into her and all her food went over her."

Josh laughed heartily. "So that's why she smelled of meatballs yesterday! Well, I can certainly see why she has you in her crosshairs."

"Yeah, she's the reason I was late for the lesson. She intercepted me and told me that she's going to make this place hell."

"Yep, that sounds like Julia alright."

"I don't know what to do. My first instinct was to throttle her, but I know that's not going to do me any good in the long run. I don't want to end up on the bad side of Headmaster Griff. I haven't built up enough credit in the bank to survive something like that."

"No, you haven't, and Julia would make sure that you're shown in the worst possible light. But she'll get bored with you eventually, you just might have to put up with some snide comments until then."

"Great, something else to worry about."

"Hey, at least you don't live here. You get to go home. It would be much worse if you were in a dorm with her."

I shuddered. "Don't give me nightmares."

"Do you have any classes now? If not I'm going to hang out with Troy and Adam; you're welcome to join us."

"That would be great, thanks. I haven't had a chance to make any friends yet. I was hoping to go outside and explore the gardens some more, if you fancied a walk?"

"Oh, that's very kind, but I try and stay away from the gardens, especially during the day. I have pretty bad allergies."

It seemed a shame that he couldn't enjoy everything the academy had to offer, especially when the surroundings were so beautiful, so I decided to explore them myself a little later. Josh took me to one of the private study rooms where Troy and Adam were waiting. Troy was taller than Josh, and had an athletic build. He had thick black hair and a wide smile. Adam's hair was longer and came down to his chin. It framed his face and hid his eyes. He wore baggy clothes and nodded towards me, instead of greeting me warmly like the other two had. We quickly fell into easy conversation and I felt at home with the boys.

I was glad to be in the company of people who actually seemed to appreciate me, and it was nice to not have to feel as though I was in some kind of competition, or under threat.

The conversation was casual as we got to know each other. We asked each other what we were studying and it turned out that Josh and I had almost exactly the same syllabus. Troy was focusing more on athletics and physical education, while Adam was more into music and art. I was excited to learn that we shared botany together though, although my excitement was short-lived when Josh revealed that Julia was in the same class.

Troy and Josh led the conversation, while Adam sat in the corner and listened, occasionally laughing along with us but he didn't really participate in the conversation. I had always been intrigued by the quiet kids; they were often the most interesting. Most people in the orphanage were like that and I got the sense that Adam had some inner pain he was hiding as well. Even though my attention was drawn more towards Josh, I found myself wanting to get to know Adam better too.

The conversation with them was enlightening. I learned a lot from them, including a lot of unspoken rules about the academy. They told me that Mrs. Thorpe wasn't as gentle as she appeared, and that I should never ever get the stroganoff to eat. Josh gave me a few pointers about the teachers I was going to have and their quirks, and I was made to feel quite at home. I also learned that Julia had been sent here by her parents who lived in Europe and she rarely went home, which in some ways made her something of an orphan too I supposed. Troy and Adam stayed for a little while, but then they both had classes to attend, so Josh and I were left alone again.

"So how long have you been here?" I asked.

"About a year. Troy and Adam started around the same time as well. We met, at the interview and just stuck together ever since. Some people stay here for longer, others just come to learn a few subjects and then leave again. It's very flexible, but it does mean that sometimes you don't get a good chance to make friends. Julia has actually been here the longest. Everyone likes to joke that she won't leave until she's studied everything, but I think it's more to do with her family situation."

"What's that?"

"Nobody really knows for sure, and Julia hasn't been forthcoming. There are rumors around, some people think that her parents are spies, others think they're royalty. Either way, Julia doesn't seem to be leaving any time soon. I think that's part of the reason why she has so much influence here. The faculty likes her because she applies herself and she always manages to skirt the rules in just the right way so that she doesn't get noticed. Personally I just think they're rich and didn't want Julia around, so they packed her off here, hoping that one day she'll be able to get a career of her own."

"That sounds pretty harsh."

"Some parents are like that," Josh shrugged.

"I wouldn't know. I'm an orphan," I said.

"I'm sorry. I didn't mean to say anything insensitive," he said.

"No, it's okay. It's nothing personal, it's just the way things are."

"What happened, if you don't mind me asking?"

"My parents died in a car crash when I was younger. I don't really remember them. I live with my guardian now," I said bluntly, trying to not give away too much information. Josh was quiet and offered me a weak smile. I'd been in this situation before. Usually when people learned my story they reacted the same way; with pity. I didn't need their pity. What I really wanted to do was tell Josh that I was a badass vampire hunter, but I had to hide that from him. He probably thought I was just sad and pathetic. I stood up abruptly and told him I was going for a walk in the garden. He blinked and looked surprised, but he didn't try to stop me from leaving.

I left, feeling stupid. Sometimes I wished I could escape my past and not have to talk about it ever again. Things had been going so well with Josh, but then they had spiraled. I didn't want to answer any more questions about my past, so it seemed the only thing to do was make a hasty retreat.

# Chapter Five

When I reached the garden I felt a little ashamed that I had rushed away from Josh with little explanation. Talking about my past always triggered me into feeling vulnerable and I often lashed out in a defensive manner. I wasn't used to making friends and, usually, when people asked me about these conversations I was ready for them to try and take advantage of me somehow. I had worked so hard to fight my way through my feelings of inadequacy, but they always managed to rear their ugly heads. They were like an infection that just wouldn't go away, much like the vampires.

Being in the garden helped relax me. From this vantage point the building looked smaller and the problems with Julia seemed smaller and insignificant. The plants had their own natural lifespan and they didn't care at all about my problems. I breathed in the fragrant aroma and felt the soft petals. I watched the bees and ladybirds flutter about. I gazed at the caterpillars crawling along the stems and lost myself in thoughts about the natural world and how peaceful it was. It was nice to spend some time not having to think about bullies and vampires, and all the evil in the world. It was a relief to be reminded that there was actually a great deal of beauty.

*

I stayed out in the garden until it was time for my next class; botany. Julia gave me an evil look when I arrived and made a point to trim one of her plants with clippers.

"What a welcome," I muttered as I settled in next to Adam. He shifted uncomfortably and turned his body in on itself as I sat down. The teacher was a bubbly woman who quickly settled into the lesson and spoke at a high pace. It was a very hands-on class, with lots of flowers around to explore and experiment with. There were also huge vines, and tomato plants. The air was humid, and sweat began to prickle on my skin.

For some reason Adam wore a hoody and I couldn't understand how he could have been comfortable in that, but he didn't seem affected by it. He just tended to his plant, snipping away the dead leaves.

"I'm glad to see you don't have allergies like Josh does," I said, trying to make conversation. This class was far more relaxed than history and we were able to talk with each other, not that Adam was too talkative initially. I hoped that some time alone would bring him out of his shell. I could imagine it wasn't easy to make himself heard when he had Troy and Josh to contend with. Both of them were outgoing and it could be hard to be heard in such cacophony.

"Allergies? Oh...yeah."

"At least you get to go into the garden when you can. Do you often?"

"Yeah. I prefer going in the night. When it's quiet," he said. I could tell I wasn't going to get much in the way of conversation out of him. I focused on tending to my own plants.

"I only took this as a bit of a lark, but I'm actually loving it. I never knew botany could be so relaxing," I said, after a while. "What made you choose it?" I knew from my time in the orphanage that everyone wanted to talk, it was just a matter of time and perseverance, and finding the right topic that would elicit a reaction.

"I like growing things. I like taking care of things. There's so much death in the world it's nice to watch something grow for a change," he said. His voice was smooth and quiet, a little high-pitched.

"I can understand that." Little did he know the grave meaning behind my words. I'd never exactly had a high opinion of the world even when I had been living in the orphanage, but once I'd been exposed to the truth that vampires existed, I was astounded by how evil the world was. There was some beauty to it, but there was also a hell of a lot of evil, as well. It festered and writhed under the surface, almost as though it was some kind of boiling disease that bubbled underneath the flesh of the world just waiting to emerge and ruin everything.

The teacher didn't seem to mind us talking. It was a relaxing lesson and I was glad to feel under less pressure than I had been in Mr. Shackleton's class. Tending the plants was an exercise in mindfulness, although it did require concentration. A few times I snipped healthy leaves away and they fell to the desk, swaying through the air. Adam smirked. His plant looked pristine.

"I hope this plant isn't angry with me," I joked.

"I think it'll be okay. They're pretty friendly here," he said, and stroked the petals of his plants. I tilted my head and looked at him curiously.

"What are you doing?" I asked.

"I'm just showing them a little bit of affection. They grow better when they know they're wanted." He immediately dipped his head in shame and I could tell that he had been ridiculed for this before. I felt awful for the scorn in my voice. "Never mind," he added. "It doesn't matter."

"No, please, go on," I said, taking a few steps to the side to be closer to him. I could smell the scent of the rose in the air. I admired his plant. The petals were full of color and the stem was straight and strong. It looked perfect. "Do you mean to say that the plants have feelings just like we do?"

"It doesn't matter. It's stupid."

"No, please," I pressed. Adam licked his lips nervously. His desire to talk about this seemed to override his embarrassment. His words tumbled out quickly, and his eyes lit up in a way that I hadn't seen them do, until now.

"Well of course they have feelings. It makes sense if you think about it. After all, they are life, just like us and just like animals. They might not be as advanced as we are or capable of complicated thoughts, but they still react to their environment, they still thirst for nourishment and nutrition, and like everything else they want to spread their seed so that they might live on through their children. They respond to care and attention. I talk to all of the plants. It helps them grow. It helps me as well. Sometimes I think they understand me better than anyone else. You probably think I'm weird."

"I admit it's something I've never heard before, but we all have our little quirks. When I was growing up I had lots of imaginary friends because all my real ones kept leaving. But what about Troy and Josh? Don't they know you better than these plants ever could?"

"They're great, but I can talk to plants in a way I can't talk with anyone else. I guess I just feel I can be myself around them. They don't judge me. They don't argue with me. They don't doubt me. They just listen. And look at how well they grow?"

He turned his body to point behind him at the rows and rows of plants in the classroom. I followed his gesture and my mouth dropped open at the sight of all the colorful flowers. There was such a mixture that I lost track of counting them. Some I recognized from my brief foray into the garden, although I wouldn't have known what species there were. I had seen them when I came in, of course, but I had assumed that the teacher tended to them, not Adam.

"You made them all grow so vividly?" I asked, astonished.

"I did," Adam's eyes gleamed with pride. "I figured I had the time to do it, so I come in here when I can't sleep. It's relaxing and peaceful. One day I want to be the gardener here and take care of all the plants."

"I think you certainly have a talent for it," I said. He smiled at me and then a shadow loomed over us. The smile faded from his face and he shrunk into himself once again, turning back to his plant. I turned to see Julia standing before us.

"Is he going on about his precious plants again? As if they're alive," she barked a laugh. "Still, it makes sense that you would attach yourself to someone like him." She wielded the clippers like a weapon. Each one of her movements was fraught with danger, as though she might have lunged forward and cut us at any moment. However, she only seemed to want to pour scorn on our conversation, as though she thought we needed her approval to be friendly. I threw a glance over to her desk where her flower sat. It was an ugly, thorny thing. The stem was twisted and the head of the flower drooped. The thorns were spiky, as though it was afraid of anything getting too close.

Adam withdrew into himself and despite my best efforts to get him to talk he wouldn't open his mouth for the rest of the lesson. As soon as it was over he rose and pulled his hoody around him, pushing the whole world away again. I couldn't understand how he could wear such a thing outside when the sun was shining brightly, but he dug his hands into his pockets and walked briskly back to the main building, dipping his head so that nobody had to see him. I looked with ire at Julia as she confidently strode out of the classroom. I didn't know what had happened in her life to make her such a vile person and I didn't much care. There were some basic standards that people should have followed and she was not paying attention to them at all. She was evil, I had no doubt in my mind of that, and I hated how she treated people. I could handle her needling me, but Adam seemed so timid and harmless. All he wanted to do was tend to his plants; there was no need, absolutely no need, for her to treat him so cruelly.

*

I left class myself and I had a bit of time that I was supposed to use for studying, but since I had only just started and didn't have any assignments yet I decided to explore the school a little more. I hoped to run into Josh again and dreaded an encounter with Julia and her cronies. As I walked back to the main building the sunlight danced on my arms. It was a nice feeling. So much of my life was spent in the shadows of the night, I liked the moments when I could enjoy the sun. It reminded me that I was a part of the normal world.

I thought about what Adam had said too, about how plants had lives and wanted the same thing as the rest of us; to endure. I wasn't sure I agreed with him about plants having feelings, although part of me was tempted to apologize to the grass I was treading on. But the rest of what he had said made sense. After all, wasn't that the driving force through life, to live? Maybe it was that simple and the meaning of life was to be alive. It was the same for vampires. That's why they did what they did. They turned other creatures so that the species could continue, and even Slayers were the same. We were taught that we'd have to have children one day to continue the bloodline and make sure the world is protected from evil. Everything just seems to keep going, as though there's no end. We're all just a link in the chain and the only point of the chain existing, is that it does exist.

I wasn't sure how that made me feel. I suppose it made me feel kind of empty, so I tried to push the thoughts from my mind. I was envious of Adam in that moment, because at least his hobby was making things grow and thrive. Although I was making the world a better place, I was doing so by killing things. I was no better than pest control really. I didn't create life or put anything of worth into the world. I just took things away.

I ended up walking through the hallways, strolling aimlessly, and my path took me to the gym. I heard the loud, squeaking echo of sneakers against the polished floor and the heavy impact of basketballs pounding against the backboards. As I entered I saw Troy in mid-flight, one arm stretched high, the ball leaving his hand and nestling into the net with a satisfying ripple. He landed and grinned, then high-fived one of his teammates. His flesh glistened with sweat and his muscles were tensed as he sprinted around the court in this practice game. He was clearly the best player on the court and I leaned against the wall, watching him with interest. I'd never been one for sports, apart from when the Olympics rolled around, but watching him caught my attention. I admired the way he used his body. It was like watching an animal whose body had been honed over years of evolution to be perfect for one purpose and one purpose alone. Everything moved exactly how he wanted it. Every step he took was measured, every movement of the arm and flick of the wrist was timed perfectly and when he had the ball it became an extension of himself.

I'm sure there were plenty of nuances to the game that I simply couldn't grasp, but I could see the talent he had and I was in awe of him.

It wasn't too long until the game ended. Troy embraced the other players as they gave each other high-fives. They laughed and left the court, soaked in sweat, eagerly grabbing towels. I noticed that I hadn't been the only one watching the game. A few other girls had taken quite the interest, and they flocked to the players, pairing off with them. Only a few, including Troy, didn't seem to be interested, although he was glad of a towel. He wrapped it around his shoulders and wiped his face. His cheeks were ruddy and his chest heaved as he panted. His loose shirt clung to him and when he saw me he smiled widely.

"You thinking of joining us?" he asked.

"I'm happy watching at the moment. I'm not sure it's my game," I lied. I could probably smash all the records of the school, if I put my mind to it, but it felt like cheating in a way. It wasn't like I was taking steroids or anything, but since I had been blessed with magic, I felt it was unfair to people who trained and worked hard every day of their lives. Plus it wouldn't help me remain stealthy. Shame though, because it looked like a lot of fun.

"Well, no matter, we always appreciate a crowd anyway."

"You look good out there. I never realized up close how intense it could be."

"Yeah," he wiped his brow again, as sweat dripped down his temples. "It's a hard workout, but it's good to work off energy."

"I'm guessing the other players are going to work off a bit more energy. I'm surprised you didn't have a lot of girls hanging off your arm," I nodded to a cluster of people that were hanging out at the edge of the court. They were giggling and flirting. Troy turned to face them and shrugged.

"Yeah, well, most of those girls just like the fact that we're a good team and they like to think that someday we're going to be rich in the NBA."

"And you're not?"

"Nah, it's just a bit of fun. I wouldn't want to play professionally. I've always felt that if you turn a hobby into a job it takes some of the fun away. I play basketball to relax, I don't want to feel stressed about having to perform or get good results."

"I can see that. Funny how people find different ways to relax. I was just in botany class with Adam."

"Oh yeah, him and his plants," Troy chuckled, but not in a mean way. "He cares for those things like they're people."

"They do mean a lot to him. It's cute, in a way. But that is, obviously, a lot gentler than what you do. Don't take this the wrong way, but I'm a little surprised you three are friends. You and Josh I can understand, you fit together, but it doesn't seem like you have very much in common with Adam."

"You'd be surprised. But we have a laugh together and appearances can be deceiving. Adam has a rough side too."

"Adam? No way," I reared back and shook my head vehemently. "I saw him with those plants. There's no way he could hurt a fly."

"You haven't seen him lose at a game. He can get pretty mean. It takes a long time to get him there, but if you push the right buttons..." Troy let out a low whistle.

"Hmm," I said thoughtfully, "then I'm surprised that he didn't explode at Julia when she came over to us and insulted him."

"He's not stupid either," Troy said, his expression changing the moment I mentioned Julia. "Going after her is bad news and you'd do well to stay away from her as well. I don't know how much her parents have donated to this place but they must have given them a fortune because she has free reign. Either that or she's been fucking Mr. Griff."

I shuddered at the thought.

"But how can she just be allowed to get away with so much? Surely others have complained?"

"Oh yeah, but Julia outlasts them all. The people who complain eventually move on, but Julia keeps on studying, so nobody ever gets very far and it's not worth the trouble to keep on complaining once you've left this place. People go on to better and brighter things. It's just easier to stay out of her way."

"But that just lets her win. Hasn't anyone ever even tried to put her in her place?"

Troy pursed his lips and nodded slowly. "There was one girl. Her name was Suzie. Julia had it out for her from day one. Every class she was in Julia pestered her. She pulled these pranks, like putting eggs under her mattress, filling her locker with dead birds, hiding her clothes so Suzie had to run across campus wearing nothing. I don't know what Suzie ever did to piss Julia off...maybe it was nothing, but Julia was relentless."

"And the faculty didn't do anything about it?"

"Oh they punished her alright. They gave her detention, but what good is that when she lives on campus anyway? Suzie was getting more and more agitated and since nothing was happening she decided to take things into her own hands. One day she just snapped. See, Julia has this thing worked down to a tee. She'll hound you until you snap and then pretend that she wasn't really doing anything bad at all. If it's not outright violence then people don't seem to care as much. But Suzie had other ideas. One day she opened her locker to see that all her books had been gnawed to shreds by a raccoon that Julia had shoved in her locker. I still remember it actually; the raccoon scampered away. Julia was doubled over in laughter and Suzie was just standing there, holding her locker door open, looking at the torn tattered paper falling out. I think all of us knew there was something different about that day. When Suzie turned around we could all sense that something had snapped inside her, all of us apart from Julia anyway, because she was too busy laughing.

Suzie just turned around slowly and didn't say a word. She walked up to Julia, grabbed a fistful of her hair, and then slammed her against the locker. Julia screamed and tried to get away, but Suzie was stronger than she looked and was relentless. Julia sprawled across the floor and Suzie kicked her against the locker again and again. We were all stunned into silence. It was awful to watch, although none of us could say that Julia didn't deserve it."

"What happened?"

"Teachers ran out to stop it. It took two of them to pull Suzie away. She was kicking and screaming. I'd never seen madness in anyone's eyes before. Then, Julia looked up and this is the thing I'll never forget. Blood poured from her mouth and she had a black eye, but she was still smiling, because she knew she had won. She'd broken Suzie, and of course Suzie was expelled for violence. It didn't matter that Julia had pushed Suzie that far."

"So Julia wasn't punished at all?"

"She was, but it was only a slap on the wrist. She was suspended for a little while, but she wasn't expelled like she should have been. She must have had a strong talking to from Mr. Griff or Mrs. Thorpe though, because she hasn't been that bad since."

"I guess I'm lucky I got here when I did then because I can tell she'd love to do that stuff to me."

"Probably. You have to wonder at what's gone on in her life to make her act that way."

"I don't know, I think some people are just rotten to the core."

Troy looked askance at me, as though he was taken aback by what I said.

"You really believe that?"

I thought about everything I'd learned about vampires. I thought about all the people they turned against their will and how their cold, undead hearts were incapable of love. I thought about the hunger-crazed monsters I'd killed and all the horror and pain they had inflicted throughout history.

"Some people are just evil. It's in their blood," I said bluntly.

So far Troy had been light-hearted, but now he turned solemn. He spoke slowly and thoughtfully. He hung the towel over his shoulder and furrowed his brow.

"I have to disagree with you there Elsa. I think people always have a choice. I know that upbringings can be hard, but you don't have to let that define you. There's always a chance for someone to be better, to chose a righteous path. The most powerful thing in this world is our freedom to choose."

I wasn't sure about that. Sometimes I think freedom is just an illusion.

"I guess we're going to have to agree to disagree on that. I think some people are lost causes and the only thing we can do is protect ourselves from them."

"I like to think there's hope for everyone," he said. He glanced around at the empty gym. The cluster of people had moved away during the time we had been speaking. "I'm going to have to shower now, but I'll catch you later, yeah? And remember, just stay out of Julia's way!"

I waved goodbye to him, but I couldn't help but think that I had disappointed him in some way. Was it really that bad to think that some people just weren't capable of changing or worth my sympathy? Maybe my opinions had been clouded by having the veil of lies pulled back, by exposing me to the truth of the world. There was black and white, good and evil. I knew that for a fact. Vampires were evil and Slayers were good. While Julia wasn't undead, she was just the same as a vampire. She was a bully, preying on the weak and vulnerable, trying to fill a void in her own life. Troy had seen how horrid she was. I didn't understand how he could think that there was hope for her after everything she had done.

# Chapter Six

I took Troy's advice and stayed out of Julia's way for the rest of the day. I spent most of my free time in the gardens, looking at the plants with new appreciation after my conversation with Adam. I saw Josh again briefly. There was an instant spark whenever we met and I could always feel a smile twitching at my lips. It was so easy to fall into conversation with him, although sadly he was rushing away to a class so we couldn't speak for very long.

As I made my way back home Josh was on my mind a lot. Well, all three of the boys were really. Each one of them was attractive in their own way and I chastised myself for being greedy. It wasn't as though I could indulge myself anyway. The life of a Slayer wasn't conducive to romance. Still, it was fun to enjoy a little thrill, thinking about the possibilities.

I had dinner with Arthur. He seemed more pensive than usual and barely spoke as we were eating. When I asked him if he was alright, he said he was just tired, but it seemed there was more to it than that. Arthur wasn't the type to keep secrets from me, so I worried that he had had some bad news from his superiors, but he wasn't giving anything away. He smiled and reassured me that everything was alright. I had no choice but to trust him.

"There is this one girl, Julia. She's a mean piece of work and it's been so hard not to put her in her place. All I've wanted to do all day is throttle her," I said, my words laced with frustration.

"I know it's not easy, but you must control your impulses. You're only made to fight vampires, not anything else," he said, as though I didn't know it already.

"I know," I pouted, "I just need to vent. She's the worst, she really is."

"Just focus on what you have to do. She is of no concern to you."

"She is when she's got it out for me. It's all over some stupid accident as well. Am I really supposed to just take it? It feels stupid that I have all these gifts and I can't teach her a lesson. I'm supposed to fight evil, yes? Well, why is that just confined to vampires?"

Arthur smirked at that. It was good to see him smile. He dabbed the corners of his mouth with a napkin. "For a moment there you sounded just like your aunt," he placed his palms on the table and looked at me sympathetically. "I know it's frustrating to not be able to use your gifts, when they come so easily to you. There are times when I wish the rules were a bit more relaxed, but they are the way they are for a reason, unfortunately."

"It's okay," I said despondently. "I'm sure that I'll get over it. I'll just go and hunt some vampires. That'll help for sure," I said.

We cleared the table and then I got ready to go out on the hunt again.

*

The night was cool and calm. The moon was high and bright. The stars twinkled and glimmered and I was eager to run through the night. I patrolled for a while, lurking in the shadows, watching people live their normal lives. I heard them come out of bars laughing, completely lost in drunken glee. I saw lovers push each other up against the wall in a rush of passion, only to disappear to a hidden place where their lust could bloom in private. I had always wondered what it would be like to feel the touch of flesh upon my own. There had only ever been one boy I'd been close to. It was a year or so before I eventually left the orphanage. Michael had been his name and we were the only two of similar age at the time, so we naturally gravitated towards each other. He wrote the most beautiful poetry and one day he let me read some. He had a beautiful soul. We spent more time together and I remember the first time we kissed. It was the first kiss I had ever had. It was chaste and innocent, just a brief brushing of the lips, and yet, it opened up something deep inside of me and I had never been the same since.

Even though I had been nervous, I was ready to give myself to him. I thought that we could find a family in each other, since nobody else seemed to be interested in taking us. He told me that I was the only person who had ever truly understood him, and I felt the same way. My heart beat rapidly whenever I was near him and we both wanted each other. We'd planned our first night together. It was going to be perfect. He was going to be perfect. I even went out and bought a pretty dress for the occasion but when I woke up in the morning I found that he was gone. Some relative had got in touch with him and he'd left without even saying goodbye. I knew in that moment what it was like for a heart to break. He hadn't even left a letter or anything. It was almost as crushing as when my parents had died and I swore in that moment that I would never love anyone ever again. It didn't seem worth the pain and anguish, but now my mind was alive with flights of fancy about the charming Josh, the intriguing Adam, and the intense Troy.

Was I crazy for being attracted to three men at the same time? Even if I was I couldn't help myself. They were all unique and I longed to expose myself to that part of life again, to feel the flush of arousal and the pull of another person. One of the worst things about being a Slayer was lurking in the shadows and watching everyone else enjoying their lives. They were all so happy, so carefree. They could live with abandon and enjoy indulging their desires. They didn't have to think about any manifest destiny or higher purpose. They could just be creatures of instinct and follow their hearts. I longed to feel the press of warm flesh against me, to have another's breath mingle with mine.

I soon grew tired and melancholy. The streets were empty. The vampires weren't coming out to play tonight. I decided that I would make my way to Angel Academy, just to see what the place was like in the evening. I had a vague idea that I wanted to sneak into Julia's room to see if there was anything I could discover that might help me dissuade her from targeting me, but I think I just wanted to be around familiar surroundings. Things were always different at night, as well. I felt that the academy had secrets that would only be uncovered during the night.

*

The building looked much different, cast in the shadow of the night. The angel fountain was even more impressive and it seemed to come alive. Everything at night seemed more magical, as though spirits were conjured and an enchantment settled across the world. It was as though the impossible could be made real. I almost expected to see pixies dancing in the sky. It did seem a bit incredulous to me, that for all the fantasy creatures that could have existed in reality, it had to be vampires. There couldn't have been something nice, like unicorns or fairies, no, it had to be the creatures of the night.

I walked around the building, careful to not set off any alarms or catch anyone's attention. The windows were dark and foreboding. The doors were shut. The grounds were devoid of life and everything was quiet. I knew up there that the people I had met were sleeping. I wondered what was going through their minds. Was Julia thinking of anything that wasn't vindictive? Were Josh, Adam, and Troy thinking about me as much as I had been thinking about them? And what about the teachers...did they care that their students were bickering?

I ultimately decided not to creep into the building as everyone was sleeping and I doubted I would be able to rifle through any drawers without disturbing Julia. I also didn't want to get a reputation as a creep, or betray my secret purpose in the world. I felt like an intruder this late at night. Nobody was supposed to be awake, but I felt more at home when I was alone. It was something I had always liked doing in the orphanage as well. It was so peaceful to have the place to myself. I could pretend that I was the only person in the world and it was freeing to not be beholden to anyone, to not have to worry about having anyone come to pick me and 'save' me from my life. Occasionally I would bump into another nun and they'd smile. Sometimes they would try to talk, but more often than not we would simply pass each other by and go about our business. The night was a time to be alone, a time to reflect on thoughts, a time to be at peace with the world. I used to love thinking about the future and what my life would turn out to be like, although I never expected it would turn out to be anything like this. Even in my wildest dreams, I couldn't have pictured myself being a Slayer. I often wondered what the nuns would have said if they knew the truth, for they were so devout in their belief. I didn't know if they would even be able to acknowledge the existence of such evil in the world.

When I first learned about vampires my skin crawled. I thought about what it would be like to be taken against your will, to have your soul corrupted and twisted into something inhuman, to have everything you were stripped away from you and be left as nothing more than a hungry husk. It was a fate worse than death and I still shuddered at the thought of being turned into a vampire, even after I had killed dozens of them. Sometimes I felt pity for them, but I never felt guilty. As far as I was concerned I was putting them out of their misery. At least here in these grounds I didn't have any vampires to worry about. I didn't have to be on watch for anything; I could simply enjoy the atmosphere and tread slowly and not have to have my fingers ready to twitch and grab a stake.

I made my way around the building to the gardens. There were soft electric lights illuminating the path and the flowers were bathed in ethereal beauty. A few fireflies danced around the lights and the open air was gorgeous as it let the stars shine down upon me. I was drawn to the flowers like a moth to a flame. The scent lingered on the air and it was intoxicating. I found the path and walked through the flowers, wishing that I knew enough about them to know what they were. Even though I had been taught well by the nuns there were a few areas in which I was lacking. I had never really explored the world of nature, so the nuns had only ever taught me the very basic flowers. But here there were some I had never seen before and they were all delightful.

And then I saw him. He stood there, motionless in amongst the flowers. It was so natural for him to be there that he almost looked like a plant himself. He reached out a hand and brushed the petals, looking almost like he was asking it to dance. I stayed there, quiet, just watching him be so peaceful and calm among his friends. A few moments later I walked forward. I tried to be gentle, but when I spoke I startled him. He jumped and turned around, panic in his eyes.

"Don't worry Adam, it's just me," I said.

"Elsa?" he looked at me with confusion. "I thought you weren't staying on campus?"

"I'm not, but I...forgot something that I had to come back for. I thought I'd take a peek at the gardens since you seemed to prefer coming here at night. I thought there might be something more magical about them."

"I just like being alone with them," he said.

"Oh, I'm sorry if I'm disturbing you."

"It's okay. I don't mind you being here."

At the time I didn't realize how significant that was. I joined him in among the plants and breathed in the vibrant scent.

"So what are these?" I asked.

He pointed to a few flowers. "These are roses, those are lilacs, and these are lilies," he said. I looked at each of them in turn. I had no idea how you were supposed to tell them apart, aside from the difference in color.

"I'm sorry about Julia today. I wish I had said something."

"It's better you didn't. It would only cause trouble. It's better to just ignore her. She doesn't understand the relationship you can have with plants. They end up being a reflection of your own personality."

"I guess that explains why hers are so thorny and why yours are so beautiful."

Adam looked away. I almost couldn't believe I had said what I did. But that was the beauty and magic of the night; you could say things you wouldn't ordinarily have the courage to say.

"Thank you," he said softly, "but you don't know me or what I've done."

"What do you mean by that?" I asked.

He sighed. "It doesn't matter. You shouldn't be here at this time of night. They don't like anyone being here who they don't expect. If they catch you, you'll be in trouble. I'm not even supposed to be out here past curfew, but nobody is going to stop me being alone with my flowers."

I was struck by how possessive he was over the plants and it brought to mind what Troy had said. I got a sense of the steely nature behind his calm façade. "Those ones are close to dying," Adam said. The moonlight caught him in such a way that he seemed to shimmer.

"How can you tell?"

"It's the way they feel." He rubbed the petals. I reached out and tried to mimic his movements, tried to feel what he felt, but I couldn't. They just felt like petals and leaves to me. As I reached out, however, our hands brushed and I felt a tingle sweep through me. He pulled his hand away abruptly. I looked up at him, catching his gaze. I closed the distance between us.

"Have you ever wondered what it's like to die?" he asked in a faltering voice. I cocked my head.

"Have you?"

He nodded. "It seems like it would be peaceful. You couldn't do anything bad then. Everything dies, eventually...everything. At least that's the way it's supposed to be. Sometimes I'm...I'm afraid I'll be here forever."

"Would that be such a bad thing?"

When he looked at me, the moon caught his eyes in such a way that they seemed to be made out of liquid.

"Wouldn't you hate to be here forever? To live the same life over and over again, to always know that nothing is special because it's never going to end. You have all the time in the world to do everything you want. That's why I like looking after plants. I can watch the whole cycle of their lives. I can watch them grow from seeds and then eventually wither and die. There's something beautiful in the way it happens. It's the way nature intended things to be."

"But it's always sad when people die before their time. I'd do anything to have my parents back with me. I never got a chance to know them. I don't remember them. Given a choice between life and death I'll choose life every time. And there are still some things that make life worthwhile, unexpected things."

I searched his eyes and wasn't sure what I'd find, but I was taken by the moment, my heart was swept away. I was back with Michael, when my heart was raw and naïve, and I gave myself to the first flush of love. I wanted to be close with Adam, to remind him that there was still so much beauty in the world. I could sense a deep sadness to him and I wanted to show him that there was still hope. Death was never the answer. It was always life. Always. So, fueled by a rush of...something, I pressed my lips against his. He was shocked at first, and this tentativeness was evident in his response, but he quickly grew into it and I found him tender and gentle. A soft murmur escaped his lips and he took my hand in his, squeezing it softly. And then, it was over, just as quickly as it had begun.

We had shared something special, and I wasn't sure exactly what had inspired me to kiss him, but I didn't regret one moment of it. He smiled shyly at me and then he turned back around to his plants, as though I wasn't there at all.

"I'll see you tomorrow," I said, but I didn't get a reply. I wasn't sure how to read him at all. I had no idea if he enjoyed the kiss or if it even meant anything to him. He was quite the conundrum, and perhaps that was part of the attraction. I was intrigued by the fact that he had a dark past. There was something he was ashamed of, but he wouldn't tell me. I made a point to ask Josh about it the next time I saw him. I wanted to stay with Adam so that I could see the world the way he saw it, to feel so attuned to the natural world, but instead, I fled. He was right, in saying, if I was caught on the grounds I would have been punished. I didn't want to jeopardize my place in the academy.

# Chapter Seven

When I returned home everything was quiet. Arthur was sleeping again, at least I assumed he was because I couldn't hear anything in the house. I passed his study and was tempted to go in again to search for what I needed, but I didn't want to risk it. He hadn't been happy the last time and I didn't want to provoke his ire. He had been pretty fair to me and there were only a few rules he expected me to follow, so I didn't think he was being unfair by suggesting that I shouldn't intrude on his privacy.

I wished there was some way to control my dreams though. I wanted to be able to bridge the connection between the present and the past, to be able to actually communicate with my ancestors. I figured there must be a way, especially at night when the lines between the real and the magical became blurred. I lit some scented candles to fill the air with lavender and then I lay in bed and calmed my breathing so it was nice and deep and steady. I put all thoughts out of my mind and tried only to think of my aunt, the woman I had never known, the one who had bestowed this destiny upon me. I thought of her features and of everything that Arthur had told me about her. I tried to summon her essence so that when I fell asleep she would be at the forefront of my mind and swim through the sea of dreams towards me.

My consciousness drifted away and I was soon asleep, but it wasn't my aunt who came to me. My dreams were alive and I was back in that mysterious castle, with the three men kneeling before me.

Suddenly the scene shifted. I was in bed, naked, my pale, voluptuous body burning with femininity. The men were around me, pressing me, suffocating me. At first I thought I was under attack and I wanted to scream again. I wanted to lash out and fight, but then I realized that it was the complete opposite. The men weren't attacking me, they were loving me, pleasuring me, serving me. I felt the rush of arousal sweeping through my blood. I heard the moans of ecstasy and felt their hands all over my body, groping and pleasuring me. My heart throbbed and pleasure pulsed through me. My body was seized with heat and then one of the men looked up. I saw his fangs. Knew him to be a vampire. This was wrong. So wrong and, yet, it felt so right. I was gripped in this paroxysm of delight. The pleasure was more intense than anything I knew was possible, than anything I had ever imagined. Their lips were upon my throat, their erections pressed into me. My hands moved, except they weren't my hands at all. There was something so erotic about the fact that I wasn't in control of any of this. I was just an observer, and intruder, and yet it felt as though I was meant to be here, almost as though I had been here before...

I felt their kisses and then lay back. The first came over me, desire in his eyes.

"Let me serve you my mistress," he said. "I exist to pleasure you." The other two supported my head, and then I felt him penetrate me. I groaned and moaned. I shivered and quaked in my sleep, tossing and turning under the covers. Blood surged within me and my body twitched. I felt him inside me, except it wasn't me, it was her, but it was so real it was almost as though I was losing my virginity. Her hands, my hands, clasped around the vampire's head and drew him in. I had no idea what was happening, why these vampires were devoted to a Slayer, it seemed so wrong and yet I could tell that this made my ancestor happy. More than happy.

Ecstatic.

Delirious.

She had been left breathless by this rampant lovemaking and in my dream the faces of the vampires suddenly turned and shifted into the faces of the men I knew. I was so shocked and it just happened for a brief moment. I could feel the dream slipping away from me. I tried to hold on, to cling onto this pleasure because it all felt so good. I wanted more. I needed more. I used all my willpower to stay in that dream, to keep the feelings vivid, but it slipped away and faded, receding into the distance, only for there to be panting again.

It was dark. Then, suddenly, a burst of light. I felt pain in my stomach. I looked down and saw blood. My hands grasped at the stake. The blood was warm and there was so much of it. This time there was screaming, and I didn't know if it was mine or hers. Her silver mirror had fallen to the ground. It was cracked, but I caught a reflection of myself. Of her. It was my aunt. She looked up. Towards her killer, but then there was another scream.

I awoke panting and breathless. My sheets were covered in sweat and my thighs were burning. I gulped in breath and thrust my hands against my stomach, afraid that the wound would have bled through to reality, but thankfully my flesh was intact. I fell back onto the pillow and let my arm fall against my head. There was so much to process; from the heady intense first dream, to the sheer terror of the second. I wanted to think only of the first dream, especially since Josh, Adam, and Troy had appeared, but my mind was on the second. My aunt had finally come to me, and I could feel she was trying to tell me something, but I wasn't sure I wanted to relive that dream again. Not to feel her death. I had seen echoes of other deaths before, but none of them had been as painful as that. Perhaps it was because she was a direct relative, or because it had been the most recent death, but I felt awful that she had been in so much pain and I hadn't been able to do anything to help. There was another feeling I experienced as well, but I couldn't quite place it yet.

I wiped my brow and pushed myself up, too afraid and drained to get back to sleep. I perched on the end of the bed and took deep breaths to compose myself. None of this made any sense.

*

After the initial shock of being in my aunt's mind had worn off, I thought more about the first dream. I had no idea how that kind of thing would come about. It went against everything we were taught as Slayers. I didn't understand how a Slayer could betray her destiny to actually take vampires as lovers, but the reflection of my own life wasn't lost on me. There were three vampires then, and now I had three men as well. It must have just been my own subconscious getting muddled up with the past, but it was chilling nevertheless. I had no idea how to broach the issue with Arthur. How was I supposed to tell him that one of my ancestors had taken part in an orgy with three vampires? I had to try and figure it out by myself, and I was pulled to his study again.

I crept along the hallway, but before I could reach the study I heard a muffled voice coming from Arthur's room. I knew there couldn't be anyone else in there because Arthur never had anyone come to visit him. I could only make out the end of the conversation.

"...no, I won't let it happen again. I promise you that. She's under control."

I furrowed my brow. What was it that he wasn't going to let happen again? What did he mean when he said I was under control? He must have been talking about me...there was nobody else he could have been talking about. My mind was running rampant and I had to make a serious effort to calm myself down because I didn't want to jump to conclusions. I had only heard the tail end of the conversation so I was missing some context. I hovered outside his door, in two minds whether to burst in and confront him or not. His study was close, but with him being awake it was risky to go in there and search for what I needed. I didn't know what to tell him or what to share with him anymore. What did he need to control about me?

I returned to my room and dived into my bed, pulling the damp covers over me. I closed my eyes and prayed that I wouldn't drown in my dreams again. For so long I had wanted to be closer to my aunt, but now that I had finally built a bridge to her I was afraid of doing so again. I never wanted to feel that sheer panic again. It flooded my mind and it completely overwhelmed the sensations of the first dream.

I thought about the kiss that Adam and I had shared, and I wondered if it would lead to anything or if it was just a secret whisper in the night that would never be spoken of again.

*

I awoke in the morning feeling a little better. My sleep had been undisturbed and I felt rested, although I was still troubled by what I'd heard. I decided the best thing to do was talk to Arthur directly. He was my mentor after all. He was responsible for my safety and he had my complete trust. I was sure that there was a simple explanation for everything I'd heard, and maybe he could help me with the dreams as well. I went downstairs for breakfast and he was sitting there with a newspaper and some toast. When he crunched, crumbs fell down onto his jacket, and he rhythmically brushed them away with a sweeping gesture.

I said good morning to him and got myself some cereal. I thought I would wait for him to bring up the matter of the phone call, but he didn't.

"I got up in the night. I had trouble sleeping," I said. He had no noticeable reaction. "Yeah...I went to get some water and I overheard you on the phone. Who were you talking to?"

"Oh, just the council. With different time zones they do like to call at inconvenient hours, but they do like their reports."

"What did you say about me?"

"Only the truth; that you're applying yourself well and you're proving yourself worthy of being called a Slayer. You're making your Aunt proud."

"I see...I couldn't help overhear a small part of it. I wasn't eavesdropping, obviously, but it was very late and noise carried through the silence. I'm sure I heard you say something about me being under control."

A strange look flickered across his eyes, but it only lasted for an instant. In fact it was so fleeting that I wondered if I had actually seen it at all.

"I don't believe so. If you heard anything like that you must have misunderstood. These walls aren't thick, and you were probably tired. I had nothing but good things to say about you. Although..." he sighed. "I wasn't sure if I should tell you this or not." He folded the paper and placed it on the table. Then, he leaned forward and pushed his plate aside. "The truth is, Elsa, that there were some members on the council who weren't too enthused about the idea of having you as a Slayer. The thing is that since there's no control as to who becomes a Slayer and what type of person they're going to be, not everyone is going to be suited, and some of them had a few reservations about your suitability. They're just concerned, but I told them they have nothing to worry about and that you're performing admirably."

I frowned. I didn't much like knowing there were people out there who were passing judgment on me without knowing me. I'd had enough of that in the orphanage with all the people turning me down because I wasn't what they had expected from a child. I was glad that the council was in Europe so I didn't have to meet them face to face. I liked the autonomy and was glad that we had a bit of freedom out here.

"I have to tell you something else as well," I said. "My aunt came to me in a dream last night."

Arthur tensed and he clasped his hands together. He tilted his head to the side.

"What did you see?" Tension was present in his voice.

"It was horrible. It was her death." My voice cracked with emotion. Arthur leaned back and exhaled deeply. He smoothed down his shirt.

"What did you see?"

"Just a stake in her stomach. Her reflection in a cracked mirror. I didn't see who killed her. I just felt...everything."

"I'm sorry you had to go through that," he said. "Reliving a death is one of the things we wish we could prevent, but the connection that runs through Slayers is something that nobody has ever been able to have control of. It was a tragedy and let's hope you never have to relieve it again."

"But that's just it. Part of me wants to, I got this strange feeling, like she was trying to tell me something. I have no idea what it could be. I want to see her again so that she can tell me what she needs to tell me."

"I don't want to be patronizing, but I'm wondering if you're projecting a little bit here. I'm not sure that's how the connection works and maybe you're looking for a message where none exists. Haven't you told me before that these echoes are pretty much random messages you get and there's no rhyme or reason to them?"

"I did think that, but maybe I just wasn't as used to getting them. I was trying to think of her before she appeared, and then she did. I know it was horrible and painful, but I really feel like there's something she wants me to know. It's just so elusive."

"Elsa, you shouldn't fixate on things you can't control. I'm sure if there was anything your Aunt wanted you to know she would have put it in the letter she left for you, or she would have told me so that I could have passed on the message. I know you've always been concerned about your fractured link with your family and I'm worried you're trying to force one where it doesn't exist. There are plenty of things to worry about in the real world without having to trouble yourself about some mystical way of communicating with people who have passed on. Your Aunt was a Slayer and what happened to her was tragic, but it did happen and we must move on. There is no going back in life. I wish that wasn't true, but it is. There are plenty of things I wish I could take back, but we have to keep moving forward and we have to try to learn from the mistakes we make."

I could tell from the tone of his voice that he wasn't interested in discussing the philosophical implications of the Slayer's lineage and how the remnants left in each Slayer might be able to transfer messages or emotions. It was something that anyone who didn't experience it couldn't understand. He knew about it in theory, but there was something so real and vivid in the dreams that gave it this authentic feeling. I wasn't going to debate it with him, but I thought he was wrong in one respect. My Aunt wouldn't have been able to give me any message if she had only thought of it moments before she died. This was the only way she could contact me, and it might have been important.

I didn't care what Arthur said, I was going to try and get in touch with her again.

"Have you been having any other echoes from other Slayers?"

"No, just that one," I lied. I wasn't about to tell him about the other dream when I was still trying to make sense of it myself. He would never talk about the possibility that a Slayer might have taken vampires in some sort of harem. But the answers were out there somewhere, and I had to figure out a way to find them. I had to get access to his books.

"I was thinking though," I said in a way that made it seem quite nonchalant, "that I'd like to learn more about my ancestors. I know you're protective of your books, but would you happen to have one that has my lineage? I thought it might make me a better Slayer if I knew what the ones who came before me accomplished. I feel as though it would give me a better grounding for the future as well. I don't want to insult you, but I think it'll be a lot different learning from a Slayer. As much as you know, you'll never know what it's really like."

"As much as I hate to admit it, this is true," he said. He tapped his finger against his chin as he considered my proposal. "One of the books that recently arrived at the library is one such book. If you like you may visit it, but please be careful because these books are delicate and if any harm should come to them..."

"Arthur, what do you think I'm going to do? I promise that I'll be careful," I said, trying not to squeal inside. I thanked him and made a point to get to the library as soon as possible.

# Chapter Eight

The library was an old building in the heart of town. I had finished my studies at the academy for the day and was glad to be discovering something about my past. The day had gone by without incident; I only encountered Julia a few times and each time she had been so far away all she could do was give me a glower, rather than any snide comments. I only saw the boys briefly and I was glad of this because I flushed bright crimson when I saw them, after their faces had briefly appeared in my dream. I wanted to speak to Adam, to talk to him about the previous night, but he was nowhere to be found and I didn't have time to search for him. I'd see him again soon and talk to him. As much as I liked him, he was his own man and I saw more of a potential of a relationship with either Josh or Troy.

Arthur had so many books he had to rent out a room at the library where he could store the rare volumes. His generous stipend from the council allowed him to do this, and the library seemed happy to have rare and obscure books in their collection. I mentioned my name and that I was a guest of Arthur and I was shown into the room. Apparently he had already called ahead and told them which book I was able to read. The others were all kept in glass cases and cabinets under lock and key. To many it would have seemed like too much fuss to keep books safe, but Arthur had explained to me that books had knowledge and knowledge had power. In the wrong hands information could be the downfall of civilizations, could dethrone kings and shift power. It was important to keep them safe, especially because if these were destroyed then all the knowledge they contained would be destroyed to, and with them would go my family history.

The librarian who showed me into the room was a small, timid man who reminded me of Arthur, if he had been in an emaciated state. He looked as though he didn't leave the library at all; his face was pale, his hair was wispy, and he spoke in a whisper that was so light I had to strain to hear it, and more often than not I just nodded along in the hope that he was saying something I should agree with. He wore plastic gloves and carefully withdrew the book from its resting place. Its cover was tattered and green. The words had long since faded. The spine creaked as he opened the book, using tweezers to turn the pages. He handed me a fresh pair of gloves and the tweezers.

"Be gentle," he said. "Too much pressure and the pages might turn to dust before your very eyes, and Arthur would not be happy."

I assured him that I would be careful. I waited for him to leave before I investigated the book myself. I didn't want anyone else to know what I was looking at. This was for my eyes only. It was my family after all; I figured that was a privilege I could afford myself. I used the tweezers to turn the pages and saw my family name etched onto the first page, although it had been spelt different; 'Karpentar'. The ink was faded and the way it was written meant I had to decipher it rather than read it. I pored over the book, breathing in the musty smell of the brown pages, listening to the book creak with the groan of centuries, like an old man who struggled to rise from his chair.

There were names of women I had never heard of before, and for the first time in my life I experienced a sense of awe at my family. Since I had been alone I never had a sense of how many people were a part of my family, but seeing them all written down in this book was amazing. Each of them was related to me. I wouldn't have been here if it wasn't for these women, and it made me think of the future and all the people who wouldn't be born if I never had a child. It was humbling and also made me feel guilty in a sense. All of these women had had full lives, but it had ended up in me. I was the last one of the line, the one that everything now depended upon, and I didn't think I could live up to them. I wondered about their lives, about their thoughts and feelings. Had they felt the same things as me? Were we bonded by more than blood? I read as much as I could, although most of the writing was faded and impossible to read.

I wasn't entirely sure what I was looking for. I suppose what I really wanted was to know which ancestor it was whom had strayed from the Slayer tradition and took vampires as lovers rather than killing them. Unfortunately, that information wasn't easy to find as it would have been buried in so much small writing, and given that it was unlikely anyone would have noted down that scandalous behavior anyway. It was more likely that this news would have been swept under the rug in the hope that it would disappear and never see the light of day again. But nobody could silence the connection between Slayers. I wondered how many had experienced the same dream I had, and if they had, would they have told their companion? Since Arthur had been surprised I assumed that either my aunt hadn't experienced the same dream, or hadn't told him about it, but since they were so close I assumed it was the former. The whole thing was shrouded in mystery and I wished I had more control over these dreams so I could actually glean the information I wanted rather than having to go by what was given to me.

However, even though the dream was vague I still had some clues to narrow it down. From the castle surroundings and the clothing I knew it was medieval times, which meant it was a long time before the bloodline spread to America. All I had to do was look back around that particular timeframe and try to see if anyone looked or felt familiar. I hoped that when I reached the right name I would feel some sort of sensation, given that I had been inside this ancestor's head, but nothing presented itself to me. I was beginning to get frustrated and had to fight the urge to frantically turn through the book because I didn't want to rip the pages apart.

Then, I found something strange. I turned one page and glanced towards the middle of the spine. A page had been torn out. There was just a serrated line where the parchment remained. I stared at it, dumbfounded for a few moments. It didn't make any sense. Arthur would never be this careless with a book, and he certainly wouldn't have accepted one that was given to him in this condition. Like he said, knowledge was power, so presumably whatever was on this page was damning, and I felt sure that it was from the ancestor I had channeled in my dreams. But why had it been torn out? And who had torn it out? Arthur was so protective of his books that he surely wouldn't have let anyone else touch them, which only left one possibility...he was the one who had torn it. But I didn't know how to handle that. If I couldn't trust Arthur then who could I trust?

With a lump in my throat I closed the book and placed it back in the cabinet. The gloves came off with a snap and I hurried out of the room, my mind swirling with paranoid ideas. Something was happening. My ancestors were trying to tell me something, but I had no idea what.

*

I didn't go home for a while, not sure what I was supposed to say to Arthur. I didn't know whether to be straight with him and tell him that a page was missing from the book. For all I knew it might have been something innocuous, but he was so careful with his books and with the phone call I'd overheard I started to suspect that something was amiss. He was so ready to brush away the memory echoes of my dreams it was almost as though he didn't want me to investigate them. But why? Was there something for my own protection, or was there something he was hiding from me?

There was still that feeling that was present in my aunt's memory as well. The more I thought about it the more I thought I realized what it was. I hated to even think the word, but if there was one I had to use to describe it, it would have been betrayal.

*

I walked around the city for a long time. I was patrolling for vampires, but only half-heartedly, as my mind was occupied. I tried to not be paranoid, but it was difficult when Arthur was so obtuse sometimes. There were certain things he withheld from me, like exactly how my aunt died, and other things about my lineage. I wasn't sure how to confront him, or even if I should. I had no allies upon whom I could call, nobody in the organization I could ask for advice. I tried to tell myself that I was being stupid because Arthur had taken care of me. What could he possibly gain by lying to me? He had only ever looked out for my wellbeing and safety, I was probably just being stupid.

And yet, I couldn't shake this niggling feeling that I was missing something. It was like a scratchy feeling at the back of my throat or an itch that just wouldn't go away. I couldn't move on from it, and I couldn't face him either. I stayed out all night, still endeavoring to find the lair of vampires that plagued this city, but I could still only find the most feral and mindless beasts that roamed the streets trying to slake their thirst for blood. I took them all out and felt good that I was saving some people from certain doom. These vampires weren't aware enough to turn anyone, they just fed and drained life from the city, leaving empty bodies behind. The trail was cold though and I had no idea how to find the masters and rid the city of their evil. There seemed to be no pattern to these feral vampires; they were spread out and I didn't know how to narrow the search. Vampires were sly creatures and they wouldn't just come out in the open for me. I had to be just as crafty as them and figure out a way to set a trap. I had to try and goad them into revealing themselves, otherwise they would just hide in the shadows and continue turning innocent people, increasing their numbers. Vampires were, on the whole, patient beings and they always liked playing the long game. They could easily distract a single Slayer with these feral beasts and not ever have to worry about engaging me in combat themselves. While I was busy cleaning up the trash they could continue with their schemes and all they'd have to do is wait for me to grow old and die, because although I was an enhanced human I didn't have an immortal lifespan.

The night had frustrated me, but it had also helped me clear my mind. I realized that no matter what was going on with Arthur and the book and the phone call, it didn't matter in the grand scheme of things. My main focus was still in trying to stop the vampires from influencing the world and hurting innocent people, so that's what I had to do, and in order to do that I needed Arthur's help.

"I was worried something had had happened to you," he said, when I finally returned just as the dawn sun was rising. There was no point staying out beyond dawn since I would never catch a vampire in the sun.

"I just wanted to blow off some steam. I had a lot on my mind."

"Did you find the library useful?"

I glanced at him, wondering if this was a test.

"It was, actually, but I wish there was a better way for me to find out about the people who went before. Most of the writing was difficult to decipher."

"It does take a trained eye to figure out these things. You seem stressed, are you sure you're going to be okay for class when you've had such little sleep? I know sometimes it can seem like you're superhuman, but you need rest just like everyone else."

"I know," I snapped, "I'm just frustrated at this whole thing. It feels like I'm not getting anywhere. These vampires are like rats. I kill twenty and then twenty more come out of the sewers and I'm not getting any closer to the ones behind all this. I'm spending my nights out there and I'm not making any progress. Surely there's something more we can do?"

"All we can do is wait and hope that they make a mistake. This is a patient business. We can't afford to be sloppy and most of a Slayer's work is to control the vampire population. I know these feral vampires aren't the masterminds but they still pose a threat to humanity and they must be stopped."

"I don't want to just be on crowd control Arthur. I want to do something meaningful. I want to actually make a difference. What's the point of doing this if it's not going to change anything? It's like we're just fighting the tide and I'm just treading water until the next Slayer comes along, and they're going to do the same thing. We have to do something to draw them out. We have to be proactive, not wait for them to make a mistake, because they're not going to make a mistake. Right now they're confident because they know we're too few to pose a threat to them. They're not going to take any risks because they don't have to. We need to force their hand, to draw them out, to make them realize that they're in danger."

My voice had risen to where I was almost shouting, which I didn't realize until I had finished speaking. Arthur waited until I had taken a couple of deep breaths to calm down. He placed his hands on his lap and considered the matter for a moment. I was sure he was going to say that we needed to stay safe and shouldn't take any risks because the vampires were dangerous. It always seemed as though the Slayers were on the back foot and fighting a losing battle, and I was tired of it.

"What did you have in mind?" he asked.

His answer took me by surprise and I blinked slowly.

"Excuse me? Do you actually agree with me?"

"I think that what you say has merit. It is frustrating to never make inroads and while we're busy doing all this groundwork they're carrying on with their schemes. I have to agree with you that they're never going to show themselves unless we force them. So I'll ask you again...what did you have in mind?"

I paused. "I have no idea. I didn't actually think you'd agree with me so I didn't think we'd get this far. I suppose we could try and send a message out and hope they got it? Or maybe we could use me as a trap...they might be tempted at the chance to get their hands on a Slayer."

As I suggested this Arthur's expression changed dramatically. His face was locked with tension and he immediately shot the idea down.

"There's no way that's happening. It's too risky."

"But you just agreed with me that we have to take a risk to get them to come out!" I protested.

"Not a risk at your expense. I'm not going to lose another Slayer so soon, especially not when there's nobody else in your bloodline. You're the last Carpenter, Elsa, you need to keep that in mind."

"But it would be a trap. We could plan it so that I'm safe and when they're lured out we spring the trap and make sure that they can't get their hands on me. We can plan it out properly so that I'm not in any danger."

"I can't risk it Elsa. I'm sorry, but the council would never let me anyway. Slayer's are precious resources. We'll have to think of something else."

I wasn't happy that the conversation ended so abruptly. For all the power I had, I was just a Slayer. I was like a beast on a leash, only released when I needed to fight. I didn't have any real autonomy in these matters and it annoyed me. I left in a huff and Arthur said we'd talk about it more when I returned, but he had already made up his mind and laid down the law. I knew there was nothing else I could do or say to make it different. The rules were there to be obeyed, but not every Slayer obeyed them. Whoever my mystery ancestor was, hadn't obeyed them, and maybe that was why her page had been torn out, because the council didn't want her setting a bad example. But maybe the rules had been in place for too long. Maybe they didn't work anymore. Maybe they needed to be broken, and maybe I'm the one that has to do it.

# Chapter Nine

I went to the academy and by the time my journey was over I had calmed down a little, but I was still in a bad mood. I wasn't very good in class either, for I was distracted trying to think about how I could lure vampires out. It was going to have to be an intelligent trap because they weren't fools and it wouldn't be easy to trick them. Mr. Shackleton was getting annoyed at me, and Josh was stifling his giggles at my seeming lack of ability to concentrate. I apologized over and over again, but Mr. Shackleton's opinion of me wasn't getting any better.

"Wow, you really know how to piss him off. I don't think he's ever going to take a liking to you now," Josh said after class.

"I know," I groaned, leaning my head back against the wall.

"Why were you so bad today anyway? What's on your mind?"

"It's nothing," I said, hating that I couldn't talk about it with him even though I wanted to.

"You can tell me. I'm not always the best with answers but I've been told I'm a good listener."

"No, it's fine, really."

"Okay," he said, and sounded disappointed. I hated having to push him away and didn't want this to become my life. He turned to walk away, presumably figuring that I wanted to be alone, but I called him back.

"Wait," I said, "it's just...I have this problem at home. Do you ever really want to do something but you just get told no? Even when you know it's a good idea?"

"I guess that's the bane of being our age. People don't give us enough credit. They keep saying we should show some independent thought, but when we do, we're scorned and get told that we should do it another way."

"Exactly! And yeah, it might be a little risky, but it's my risk to take. I'm just so frustrated that sometimes I seem so powerless."

"Yeah, I get that a lot."

"You do?"

"Of course, I mean, I live here for goodness sake," he spread his arms out wide to gesture to the school. "It's not like I get much freedom. We have a curfew and lots of rules. Sometimes I just want to run away, so I know what it's like to live as a free man."

"Why don't you?"

His head dipped and he shrugged. "The world is a big place. It's easy to get lost out there. As bad as this place is, at least it's home. It's familiar. I know I'm safe here. But I'd say if you really believe in yourself then you should go for it and do what you like. It's easier to ask for forgiveness than permission after all," he said.

I smirked. It was a good saying, although I wasn't sure forgiveness would be forthcoming.

Unfortunately, our conversation was cut short as Josh had to get to another class, but before he left he invited me to a game later.

"Game? What game?" I asked in ignorance. Apparently Troy had a game of basketball against another academy. It must have been what he was practicing for. I nodded my head enthusiastically, eager to see Troy in action and spend some time with Josh too. He said that Adam was going to be there as well. I wondered if Adam had told Josh and Troy that we had kissed. He didn't strike me as the gossiping type. I wanted to speak to him first anyway to see exactly where things stood. I asked Josh where Adam was, making an excuse that I needed to talk to him about something in botany class. Josh said that Adam was in his room.

*

It was my first time visiting the dormitories and I felt like something of an intruder. The hallways were lined with rooms and most of the doors were open. The soft hum of conversation and music drifted through the hallways. Some of the rooms had large gatherings of people. Some of the doors had signs on them. There were notice boards throughout the corridor with various policies and advertisements on them. I walked tentatively, wondering what it would have been like to live here instead of staying with Arthur. It seemed like a thriving community of its own, just like the orphanage had been.

I passed one door that had a large notice on it saying that entrance was by invite only, by order of Julia. I snorted and shook my head. She acted as if she was royalty or something. I didn't care how important her parents were, someone needed to take her down a peg or two.

Adam's room was just a few doors down from Julia, who was thankfully nowhere to be seen. I would have been quite happy had I not seen her for the rest of the semester.

Adam's door was ajar. It was dark; the curtains were drawn and the only illumination came from the flickering light of his lamp. I knocked lightly and called out my name. I stepped in and heard shuffling as Adam rose from his resting position to sit upright on the side of his bed. He looked surprised to see me. Given the state of the room I got the impression that he didn't get many visitors. Clothes were strewn everywhere. The room smelled musty, as though he never let fresh air in, and it was cluttered with small trinkets and ornaments.

"Elsa?"

"I hope you don't mind me dropping in." I closed the door behind me and went towards the curtain. "It's so dark in here I can barely see you. Do you mind if I open a curtain?"

"Just a little, my eyes are sensitive. I prefer the dark," he said. I opened the curtains a crack. A shaft of sunlight spilled over the carpet and I immediately felt the warmth. Adam stayed on the bed, lurking in the nook he'd made for himself. Specks of dust hung in the air and I shook my head. The nuns at the orphanage would never have stood for this level of cleanliness, but I wasn't here to lecture him about that.

"I wanted to talk to you about the other night," I began. Adam's head dropped.

"I figured you would. It's alright, you don't have to say anything. As far as I'm concerned it never happened. It might as well have been a dream, given that it happened at night in the garden. I just like being with my flowers anyway. I'm not so good with people."

"No, Adam, that's not what I wanted to talk to you about at all. I'm not ashamed of what happened. It was nice. I just...I wondered if you wanted to spend some more time in the garden...just the two of us?"

"Nobody has ever asked me that before," he said, blinking at me.

"Well, I'm asking now."

He licked his lips and I wondered why he had to take so long to consider my proposal. It seemed like a simple thing to answer.

"I don't think that's such a good idea Elsa. I mean, I enjoyed it and you're...well, you know. I just...I'm not the best with people. I like being with my flowers. I understand them and they understand me. It's...uncomplicated. Being with other people makes my head hurt and I...I've hurt people before. I don't want to hurt you."

"You won't hurt me Adam. I'm not saying we should jump into anything. I just think you're cool and interesting, and I'd like to spend more time with you."

"I can. As friends. With the others. But I don't think it's a good idea for us to be in the garden together anymore."

I felt a flush of disappointment. An awkward silence descended on us. There was nothing else I could say, really. It wasn't like I was going to force him to spend time with me, I guess I was just a little disappointed that it had turned out like this. I thought I was getting through to him, but he seemed to be in a world of his own. Maybe it was best that he stayed with his flowers. However, I was really interested to learn who he had hurt and how.

I was about to leave when he asked me to close the curtains, to which I obliged him, but when I opened the door Julia was passing and shook her head. She barely took one look at me before she marched off with her cronies in tow. Angelica looked at me with the same level of derision as Julia had, while Aaron and Tommy briskly walked behind in the girls' wake. Now, although Julia hadn't done anything to directly offend me this time I was still annoyed at all the other times she had treated me with such disdain, and I hated the way she walked by me without so much as a hello. She didn't have to like me, but she could at least be civil, and I wasn't in the mood to let this go without saying something.

Julia got away with far too much in Angel Academy and nothing was ever going to change if people didn't stand up to her. I wasn't going to get violent, but I also wasn't going to let her get away with behaving like this. She had to realize that she didn't have free reign over everyone in the school and she couldn't treat people as though they were just objects destined to distract her.

I marched out of the room and walked past Aaron and Tommy. Julia and Angelica made a beeline straight for Julia's room, but just as she was about to open the door I cleared my throat. They both looked back. I put my hands on my hips and glowered at her.

"What do you want?" Angelica sneered.

"I want to ask why you gave me that look back there. You know, there's a way to treat people with respect and I don't care if you don't like me, but I'm tired of the way you're treating me. I'm sorry that I crashed into you that first day, but that's no reason to hate me, and you can't just walk around here treating everyone like they're beneath you. You're not special. You're just like the rest of us and there's no reason we can't all get along. Stop treating people like shit."

"This really isn't the time," Angelica warned, but my hackles had risen and all the frustration had boiled over. Julia still had her back to me and I was even more annoyed that she didn't seem to deem me worthy of her attention.

"Oh yes, it is time. It's long past time," I said. I pushed past Angelica.

"Seriously Elsa, just leave it," she said, but nothing was going to stop me from getting to Julia. I forced Angelica out of the way, who was no match for my Slayer strength (at this point I wasn't caring about hiding myself. I figured one hefty shove wasn't going to be enough to give anything away). I reached out and grabbed Julia's shoulder, twisting her around. I was just about ready to rant at her and give her a piece of my mind, but when she turned around I saw the tears in her eyes. Her makeup ran down her cheeks and left dark trails, her cheeks were red, and she was shaking. The entire corridor had been roused by the commotion and now saw her utterly vulnerable.

"What's wrong?" I asked, taken aback by the sight of Julia like this. I wasn't even sure if she was capable of showing any emotion other than anger. Her hands curled into fists and I thought she was about to scream, but then she spun on her heels and walked into her room, disappearing from view.

"She just found out her parents died. The last thing she needs is you having a go at her. You really pick the right time don't you Elsa? Just leave us alone. Nobody wanted you to come here," Angelica said. She and the two boys followed Julia into the room and slammed the door behind them. I was left crestfallen. I looked around, but nobody offered sympathy and I didn't know exactly what to do. It was just a case of bad timing, but I felt the pain more than most.

I hung my head and left the dorms. Part of me wanted to knock on the door and apologize, but I knew Julia wouldn't want to see me. I didn't care how much of a bitch she was, nobody deserved that.

*

I was feeling numb when I reached the gym. Josh waved to me and I sat by him. I ran my hands through my hair and he could see that I was shaking. I told him what had happened and he let out a long rush of breath.

"I mean, it wasn't your fault. You weren't to know."

"I know that," I said, "I just can't believe I put my foot in it that badly. I just had to go on the crusade and try and fix something that didn't need fixing. God...I feel like such a fool. As if she needed another reason to hate me. I want to apologize, but I know she's not going to accept it. If someone had done that to me when I found out my parents died I don't know what I'd do."

"I wouldn't think about it too much," he said.

"How can I not?" I asked. The more I thought about it, the more my soul ripped open inside me. I had never been perfect, but I had always sworn that I would never be cruel to anyone who had been through the same thing I had. "Here I go again, charging into something without thinking, I'm just a fool. I should never have gotten involved. I should have just let things lie."

"It was good that you got involved, it was just unfortunate timing," Josh said.

His words didn't provide me with reassurance though. We were sitting on the bleachers in the gym. People were swarming around us, filtering in to enjoy the game. A few players were on the court warming up before the match. The cheerleaders were stretching and making their final preparations before their performance. A few teachers stood by the sidelines and marshaled everyone around. A few people stared at me, having witnessed what just happened. I wanted to crawl away somewhere dark and damp and just push everything aside. There was a lump in my throat that wouldn't disappear no matter how hard I tried to swallow and I began to tremble. Josh sensed that something was wrong and he put his arm around me. I was suddenly enveloped in his warmth and his strength. It was as though somehow he transferred it to me. He squeezed tightly and my head rested against his shoulder. His body was steely and strong, comforting and manly. I closed my eyes and for a moment all my troubles seemed to drift away as though they were being carried by a summer cloud. All I wanted was to turn back time just for an hour or so and stop myself from making such a mistake.

"She's never going to forgive me for this," I said, eventually. "She's never going to forget it. I know I wouldn't."

"You don't know what's going to happen. She might have to go back home. There's no sense in worrying about anything until it happens, especially when it's out of your control."

Arthur had said similar things to me. They were difficult to remember though. Even though I was a Slayer I was still just a teenage girl with all my flaws and fractured mind. All the difficulties of my youth came flooding back. Every conflict with another child affected me greatly, because they always moved on, by literally moving on. They always got picked by a family, but I didn't. I stayed at the orphanage and it always felt as though I was being punished for being naughty, like somehow all the adults knew I was too wicked to be a part of a happy family.

And now I felt the same thing. This academy, with all its children and its dorm rooms, felt like the orphanage. I knew deep down it wasn't, but it didn't help me either way. And now Julia was an orphan. I remembered what Troy had told me about Suzie. I didn't know if I was going to be able to stop myself from fighting back, if Julia really came at me and wanted revenge. I could see everything slipping away, crumbling before my eyes. I could see myself being thrown out of the academy and then where would I be? With Arthur; fighting an endless fight against the undead and no hope of anything changing any time soon.

I think Josh sensed that he wouldn't be able to say anything to make me feel better. We sat there quietly. I sensed a few murmurs from people passing by. Word spread quickly around here, and soon everyone would know what I had done. I longed for the game to begin, just to give me some distraction. There was a sudden hush, but when I looked up through blurred vision I didn't see the teams on the court. Instead, I saw Mrs. Thorpe standing at the entrance of the gym, and she was looking directly at me.

Mrs. Thorpe raised her hand and beckoned with one finger for me to join her. Everyone knew she was pointing at me, and I wasn't the only one to have seen her.

"Oh God..." I moaned as I stood up, having no choice but to face the inevitable.

"You'll be okay. It was just an honest mistake," he said. As I rose his hand slid around my waist and arm, and before I left his company he squeezed my hand tightly. It felt nice, and I wished so badly that I could have just stayed in his arms. I wanted to curl around him and enjoy the feeling of his body around me. I wanted to melt into him, but instead I walked away, alone, as I ever was.

# Chapter Ten

I'd never felt more self-conscious than when I walked down the bleachers. I heard people whispering as I passed, but I tried to hold my head high. I looked back at Josh, who was now sitting there all alone. I regretted that I had to leave him, and that I wouldn't get to see Troy in all his glory. With each step I took tension increased and a knot of anxiety twisted in the pit of my stomach. It seemed stupid that I should feel so vulnerable. I was a Slayer. I could fight and kill creatures of the night, and here I was, trembling at the thought of a scolding from a schoolmaster.

I had been warned that Mrs. Thorpe wasn't as nice as she seemed, although I hoped that was an error and she was just as friendly as the first time I'd met her. There was a look in her eyes that told me otherwise. She didn't say anything to me. As soon as I reached her she turned around and strode away, expecting me to follow. I walked along in her wake, sullen and worried. The crowd that streamed in for the game parted before us and I had a feeling I would soon become infamous.

We went to her office, which was near reception.

"Close the door behind you and take a seat," she said. Her desk was wide and a computer monitor was angled at the edge. The window looked out to the gardens and I saw a few people enjoying the aroma of the flowers; evidently not everyone was interested in basketball. I was too worried to look around Mrs. Thorpe's office properly. She looked as prim and proper as ever. She clasped her hands together and placed them on the desk, leaning forward slightly.

"I assume you know why you're here," she said in clipped tones. I nodded numbly, not sure what to say in my defense. Julia was the darling of the faculty. I should never have let things get the better of me. I should have just left it.

"It was just a mistake. I didn't know that her parents died."

"That's not really the point though is it Elsa? The simple fact is that students of this academy do not go around accosting people and demanding things from them. I know that Julia can be difficult sometimes, but if you lose your temper at the first sign of trouble you'll never get very far in life. I told you there are expectations at this academy, high expectations, and so far you are failing to meet them."

"I'm trying my best. I really am. I just...it seems so unfair the way she treats people and gets away with it. I wanted to talk to her so that things might change for the better. I thought maybe I could talk some sense into her, but I just happened to choose the wrong moment," my voice trailed off at the end, growing weaker.

"Yes, you did. The way you acted was certainly not conducive to a rational discussion."

"What's going to happen now? Am I going to be punished?" I asked.

"I don't think that's necessary, this time, but you have to watch your behavior because we will not tolerate it anymore. This is between you and Julia, so you have to go to her and apologize. We'll all be keeping a close eye on you, though, Elsa, and if you slip up again, this place clearly isn't for you, which would be a great shame. Now, go and apologize to Julia."

"Yes Mrs. Thorpe," I said. I quickly pushed my chair back and left the office as quickly as possible, worried that the longer I stayed there the more likely it was that a worse punishment would befall me. I hurried through the empty hallways. The passionate sounds of the basketball game echoed out from the gym. I heard a raucous cheer and wished that I was a part of it, but I had to go and face the wounded animal. Julia was spiteful enough when everything was rosy in her world. I dreaded to think what she was like in her current state.

*

The dorm rooms were so quiet compared to earlier. It was as though I had stepped into a ghost town. My throat was dry and I felt light-headed. I reached her door. The foreboding sign warned me not to enter unless invited. There was an aura around the room, pushing over people away. I tentatively knocked, softly. For a moment I was afraid it was too soft and I didn't know if I had the courage to knock again. The door opened. Tommy stood there. The room was dark, just like Adam's had been. Even though Tommy answered the door it was Angelica who addressed me.

"What do you want? Haven't you already done enough today? I hope Mrs. Thorpe has already spoken to you because it's better that people like you don't get to be here. You should just go."

"I just want to apologize to Julia," I said humbly, hating that I had to come to her like this. I peered through the darkness and tried to see where she was, but they all blended into the shadows and it was difficult to see past Tommy, who did his best to block the door.

"She doesn't want your apology. She doesn't want anything from you. Just go and leave us alone."

I wasn't about to be deterred by Angelica. I decided to just ignore her, say my piece, and then leave.

"Julia, I'm sorry for what happened. I know how you're feeling. Like everything has been ripped away and you have nothing solid to stand on. I just want you to know that if you need anything I'm here to talk."

Angelica snorted with derision and Tommy sneered at me. I waited for a response from Julia, but when none came I turned away. I had done what Mrs. Thorpe asked, although I knew the worst was to come. As soon as Julia recovered I was going to feel the full brunt of her wrath and she was going to torment me and hound me until I broke.

But just as I was about to leave their earshot I heard a small voice.

"Leave us alone," Julia said. Her voice was rasping. I thought she was talking to me at first, but then Angelica turned and questioned her.

"Elsa. I want to talk to you," Julia said. Angelica protested emphatically, but Julia wasn't having any of it. "GO!" she yelled, and her three companions scurried past me. Angelica shot me a look of hatred, although I could tell that she was confused as well. Frankly, I was too. I crept into the dark room and as I grew closer I could make out Julia's shape sitting on the floor with her legs folded. The curtains were open just a crack, and a sliver of sunlight ran through the middle of the room, ending just before it reached her. I closed the door behind me and sat down on the floor with her.

For a long time we sat there in silence, not saying anything. Then, she opened her mouth.

"You lost your parents when you were very young didn't you?" she asked.

"I did."

"Did you grasp then what it all meant?"

"Not really. I was confused about how exactly it had happened. Part of me thought that they just needed to get better, but I remember feeling empty inside. As I got older I understood more of what it meant. I felt so alone. My connection to the world had been severed. My parents were the people who were supposed to help me understand the way the world worked and to guide me through life. They were supposed to teach me, but there was just a hole where they should have been. The thing I've always hated is that I was denied the chance to know them."

"I never knew my parents. Not really. They sent me away to boarding school when I was younger, and then when they had the opportunity they sent me here. I always felt like I did something wrong and nobody told me what it was. Even when I was home for the holidays they treated me like a guest rather than their daughter, and I never understood why. Why would you have a child if you didn't want to love and cherish her? Why not just put me up for adoption so that I could actually be a part of a loving home?"

"It's not that easy to get adopted. You might have been like me and be raised by nuns."

"It can't have been that bad. At least the nuns cared for you."

"Yes, they did, but it hurt every time parents came to the orphanage and they picked everyone apart from me. I grew older, and the older I got the more chance I knew that I wouldn't be picked. At least your parents cared enough to give you a good education and a good grounding in life. It can be hard though, knowing that there are always things left unsaid. There are so many times I wish I could have one last conversation with them, even if it only lasted a few minutes, just to say goodbye to them or tell them that I love them."

"I don't know what I'd say to them if I ever saw them again. I'd probably just ask them why they treated me the way they did. I don't know if I'd like the answer though. But now I'll never get to understand them."

"How did it happen, if you don't mind me asking?"

"They were driving across a mountain range in Europe. The road was icy and dangerous. A truck came the other way and its tires lost grip. It swung around and knocked them into the side of the mountain."

"My parents died in a car crash too," I said solemnly. Silence lingered around us for a few moments.

"You know, I don't hate you," Julia said.

"You could have fooled me." I could sense a kind of kinship growing between us. We shared something deep and solemn, something few people could understand. Back in the orphanage we had all shared the same thing and even if we hadn't liked each other there was still a bond between us, as we had all lost something precious. In this room, in this moment, I felt as though I could ask Julia anything. "Why do you do it? Why do you try and antagonize so many people?"

My eyes had adjusted to the dim light to such an extent that I could see the change in expression on her face. She looked almost apologetic.

"The stupid thing is that I don't really know. Do you ever think that sometimes we get these roles thrust upon us? When I started here I was just the same as anyone, and I hated it. I hated being a part of the crowd. I wanted to stand out, and there were a few people who annoyed me. I decided that I wasn't going to stand for it. I wanted to get what I wanted and I wanted to stand up for myself, so I started to push back, and I suppose I decided I'd see how far I could take it. I charmed the faculty and made sure I took calculated risks. It was easy when I actually did it, and I found that I soon had the run of this place. I can do whatever I want and people listen, and I don't have to put up with crap."

"But what about when it goes wrong? What about when you push people too far? Like Suzie?"

At the mention of Suzie's name I saw Julia visibly flinch.

"I did go too far then. It's like a drug. You push and push, and you keep wanting to see how far you can go, and then something snaps. I hated that day. I feel bad for her. I was too hard on her and I wish I could go back and change things, but I can't. But then everyone thought that Suzie got expelled because of me and that added to my aura I guess."

"If she didn't get expelled because of you, then why did she leave?"

"She was ill. They were thinking about taking her out of the academy anyway. There's a lot that people don't know. Like a lot of people think I have the run of this place but I don't really. I got into major trouble for what happened with Suzie. I had all of them yelling at me, telling me how this wasn't how members of the academy behaved, how I had to read the code of conduct again and make sure I learned it by heart. I suppose, really, that's the only thing I have to thank my parents for; their donations to this place helped keep me here. But one of the reasons I've been here for so long is because they wiped my credits because of what I did to Suzie. They don't let me get away with anything at all. I had to redo everything."

"Why don't you tell people this?"

Julia scoffed. "Because it would ruin my reputation. I don't want to be like normal people. I don't want everyone else to know I'm struggling. Why do you think I'm staying in here? The only reason I'm talking to you is because you've been through the same thing and it actually helps to have someone who understands. But don't think this means we're going to be friends. As soon as you walk out that door we go back to the way things were. To be honest I don't even want to talk about it. I just want to be with someone who knows, you know?"

"I know," I said. And I did know. One unspoken rule that arose in the orphanage was that you never pressed anyone about their childhood or their tragedy, if they didn't want to speak about it. It was enough, knowing that something had happened in the past. Some people didn't like revisiting the gritty details, and some would rather try to pretend and forget that anything had happened. I still didn't like Julia even though I understood a little better why she acted the way she did. Part of it was simply because she was allowed, and while I hoped that this incident would adjust her behavior I didn't hold out much hope.

I wasn't sure what else to say, but at least I had apologized like Mrs. Thorpe had wanted. It was the first real conversation I'd had with Julia as well, and it was nice to have a momentary peace treaty.

"Does it ever get any easier?" she asked.

"Eventually, in time. There are good days and bad days. Some days the good ones are really good, and other times the bad ones are really bad. Sometimes you can go months without thinking about it and then it'll hit you like a juggernaut and you're right back at the moment where you found out. It's like no time has passed at all. I think you just learn how to cope with it, how to move on."

Julia nodded. I stayed there for a few moments longer in case she needed to talk about anything else, but she was as silent as Adam. I rose and left the room, knowing that as soon as I did we would go back to our old dynamic. I offered one last apology, but this time it wasn't an apology for what I had done, it was an expression of sympathy at her plight. It had always seemed wrong to me that a child had to be without their parents.

# Chapter Eleven

I left Julia's room with mixed feelings. I didn't think anything was going to change, even though I had a better insight into her behavior. At least I had gotten rid of the knot of anxiety that had twisted like a knife inside me. As I walked down the corridor, I passed Angelica and the two boys. She scowled at me and quickly returned to Julia's room, probably eager to discover what we had discussed. She might have even been afraid that I was going to take her place, not that that would ever happen.

I turned a corner and was surprised to see Josh leaning against the wall. He pushed himself forward and flashed me that charming smile of his.

"What are you doing here?" I asked.

"I thought I'd come and see how you got on. I figured Mrs. Thorpe would want you to apologize. She's quite big on people making up for their mistakes, and I thought you might need to see a friendly face when you came out."

"But the game?"

Josh shrugged. "It's not the first game I've seen, and it won't be the last. Besides, it wasn't a close thing. The game was basically over in the first quarter. So how was it in there?"

I glanced over my shoulder to make sure that nobody else was in earshot and then nodded forward. We walked towards one of the secluded cloisters so we could have a bit of privacy. "It was strange really. I apologized. At first I didn't think she was going to listen to me, but then she ordered the others out and she wanted to speak to me alone. It's not easy to understand the pain. She just wanted someone who knew what she was going through to sit with her."

"Is this the beginning of a beautiful friendship?"

"Oh no," I shuddered, "not at all. She made it quite clear that nothing was going to change, nor would I expect it to. Give her a few days and she'll be back to normal I'm sure."

"Did she say if she was going to leave?"

"I don't think so. This place is her home really. It's quite sad; her parents basically shunned her and put her into boarding school and then this place. I don't think she's ever had a place apart from school that she can really call home. Her parents don't sound like nice people."

"No...I've always assumed that when I have a kid I'll want to spend as much time with them as possible."

"You want kids?"

"Yeah, I think so. It would be fun, I think, to teach someone and watch them grow and learn from their mistakes. If I get the chance that is," he added, looking sheepish.

"I think that's nice. I have to have a kid one day even though I'm not sure I really want one, at least I can't imagine having one just yet," I said carelessly. I didn't even realize my slip up until he pointed it out.

"What do you mean you 'have' to have kids?"

My eyes widened in panic and my mind worked quickly to try and cover for my mistake. "I just meant because I'm the last of my family. I never had any brothers, or sisters, or cousins, so I feel like I have a responsibility to try and keep things going. I feel like I owe it to my parents since they never got the chance to have any more kids."

"It's like Adam says, the purpose of life is to spread more life. It's not very romantic, but it probably has more than a grain of truth to it."

"Yeah...I was talking to him the other day in class and to Troy as well. What happened with him? He said that he hurt someone in the past, and Troy said that he's not as gentle as you might think."

Josh seemed to be considering whether to tell me more or not. "I'm surprised that Adam told you that much to be honest. He doesn't like talking about the past. Well, he doesn't like talking much at all, really. I suppose there's no harm in telling you. It's not like it's a secret, he just doesn't like reliving it. I keep telling him that it was just a mistake and that people always make mistakes. He's not the only one." He inhaled sharply. "Basically there was someone he liked a few years ago. He was young, naïve, didn't really know how these things worked. I think he assumed that because he felt such strong feelings for her that she would return them. It seemed natural to him, and sure, she liked him and was friendly with him, but she didn't have the same type of feelings. Adam couldn't understand this. He thought if he just tried to show her and proved to her the depth of his feelings that she would understand. He couldn't seem to grasp that she knew exactly how he felt, she just didn't feel the same way. But, he wanted her badly, and he tried to convince her, and he ended up scaring her away. She screamed and basically tore herself away from him, and he hates thinking that he could ever have driven anyone to be so scared of him. Adam is a very sensitive soul and he takes things personally. He's never been able to get over that."

"Oh," I said. Somehow I had expected something more.

"He'll get over it eventually, but for the time being he's happy with his plants."

"And what about you? Are you wise in the ways of romance?"

"Is anyone?" Josh answered We both laughed. "I don't know...I guess I'd like company, but there are some things...I'm not sure I really know myself yet. I feel like I should understand myself before I get with another person. It just seems like it would get complicated otherwise."

"I guess part of a relationship is getting to know yourself as well as the other person."

"Maybe, but...so many things change during these years. Do you ever go through something and wonder if you're a completely different person than you were before? Like...I barely remember my early childhood; am I the same person I was back then? Am I going to be the same person as the one I'm going to grow into? What makes me 'me'?"

"I suppose memory is a part of it, but also aspirations and dreams and your passions. I know what you mean about going through something big. I felt like I changed so much in the orphanage and then..." I wanted to talk about my transition into being a Slayer, but I had to cloak my meaning in vague terms. "Things happen and you grow up. You start to see the world in a different way and you have to change your beliefs. Sometimes I don't know if we're ever truly 'one' person. People see different aspects of us. We hide different sides of us from different people. I wonder if it's ever possible for one person to know everything."

"Maybe it's for the best that they don't. Some things are best kept secret. A little mystery is always good. It keeps things interesting," he said. I certainly agreed. It pained me that I had to keep my whole life as a Slayer under wraps from him. I wanted so badly to tell him, to ask him for advice and guidance, and to share this part of me but I couldn't. It had to remain secret, and there was a part of me that thought he might be holding something back from me as well. My confidence had been knocked a little, after Adam had told me he basically didn't want anything to do with me, although knowing the truth behind his behavior helped alleviate some of the suffering. Josh seemed so confident and easygoing that I assumed he'd ask me out if he really wanted, and I figured he might just be being friendly to me. I wasn't ready to assume anything, especially not in the area of romance where I lacked experience.

Whenever I was around him, I couldn't help but think about the dream I'd had where his, Adam's, and Troy's faces had replaced the vampires around me. Heat instantly flared inside me and I began to squirm, feeling a twitch between my legs. I wanted him so badly to ask me out, or to kiss me, or to do anything. I'd never been this desperate for anything before, but all we did was talk. I left, feeling disheartened, wondering if I was ever going to be blessed in romance or if I would always be forlorn and lonely.

# Chapter Twelve

The following week went by without incident. Julia was absent from classes as she was grieving and I didn't encounter Angelica, which was a blessing. It actually made the week pass by rather quickly. I had almost forgotten what it was like to live without stress. I was able to concentrate on classes and actually had some praise from Mr. Shackleton. I spent more time with the boys, although we only talked and nothing happened on the romance front. My mind was still alive with the dream I'd had, although since that last dream I hadn't had anymore and was left to nourish myself on the images and sensations that lingered in my body. It was darkly exciting though, to have these thoughts while in their company. Josh was right in a way, that some secrets were exciting to have, and when I returned home I was left breathless and flustered.

Hunting vampires did a lot to quell my frustrations, but Arthur and I had still made no progress in our efforts to tempt the master vampires out from their lairs. Every idea I had was flawed, and Arthur wouldn't approve anything that wasn't perfect. I was tempted to go ahead without him, but I couldn't bring myself to do it, not after everything he had told me about the strict council and how dangerous it was. Even though I was confident in my abilities as a Slayer the simple fact was that I was still inexperienced. I had only ever gone after feral vampires, not the more powerful ones, and I didn't want to be caught out of my depth.

There had been no progress in anything else either. I waited every night to experience another dream, but my ancestors didn't come to me and I wondered if Arthur was right and the images I'd seen had just been random assortments of echoes without any rhyme or reason to them. I wanted to believe so badly that they had significance, but if they did then why were they silent now? I didn't ask him about the book. I decided that I had been paranoid and things at the academy were getting the better of me. Arthur hadn't ever done anything to put me in danger. Everything he'd done had been to look out for me and it was ungrateful of me to think otherwise. He was evidently under stress from the council and I didn't want to give him anything else to worry about. We just had to be patient. I was still young and I, hopefully, had a lot of life left in me. Everything would come in time, I just had to wait for it. I had to be patient like the vampires were. It was probably the only quality about them that was worth admiring.

Julia's tragedy had got me thinking about my own parents and how I had neglected thinking about them for a while. It was too easy to let them slip into the ether. I had a link to my aunt, but there was none to my Mom and Dad. I wished that I could have done something to bridge the gap between this world and the afterlife, and I started to become melancholy. I tried to hide my mood from the people around me, but they picked up on it. Josh was caring and asked me what was wrong, Troy tried to cheer me up, while Adam was just his usual quiet self. I told them that I missed my parents and they sympathized with me, but there wasn't much they could do to help my mood. Arthur tried his best, as well, but he wasn't attuned to that kind of thing. Funnily enough, the one person who could have helped most was Julia, but I certainly wasn't going to ask her to help me out.

While I was out on patrol I was struck by how many people were falling in love and enjoying human coupling. I suppose it was one of those things where it was on my mind, so I was seeing it more often than I usually would, but everywhere I looked it seemed as though people were pairing away and while I was jealous there was also a part of it that I didn't understand. I didn't know how anyone could limit themselves to just one person when there was so much variety to be had. Josh, Adam, and Troy each had unique qualities that made them special and there was no way I could have just chosen one, if I was forced too.

Not that it mattered anyway, although there was one day when they were sweet and invited me for a midnight picnic in the gardens to cheer me up. I was a little annoyed that it was so late, but they said they wanted to do it at midnight because Josh's allergies were less sensitive, and Adam always preferred to be in the garden at night when it was calmer and he could be sure of having the place to himself. I readily agreed because I wanted to spend time with them and it sounded pretty magical to be in the garden at midnight, but it was frustrating that it was at the academy. So much of my life revolved around the place. Part of me wanted to escape.

*

When the night came I was filled with nerves as I approached the academy. I wasn't entirely sure what to expect. It was so magical that it almost seemed like a date, but I wasn't sure if that was what they intended. I was taking a night off from patrolling and I hoped that no feral vampires would kill anyone. I wore a loose dress as the night was warm and I never felt the cold anyway. The stars were bright, as before, and as I skulked around the garden I heard their muffled voices. They were in a secluded part of the garden, far from the building, and I hoped that it would keep us hidden from any prying eyes so we could enjoy a good few hours together without interruption.

They all looked good and relaxed, as though they were in their natural element. They welcomed me with open arms, although Adam was a little distance away, focused on his flowers. They had laid out a picnic blanket for us to use and had smuggled some sandwiches, chips, and drinks out of the academy. Troy gestured for me to take a seat and so I smoothed my dress out and folded my legs beneath me, settling on the blanket. The air was cool and I felt comfortable under the stars.

"I hope this is alright. We know you've been feeling down. Hopefully your troubles will start to get further away," Josh said.

"It was a shame you had to miss the game. I made the shot of my life," Troy said, bouncing on his heels as he reenacted the shot.

"I appreciate all of this. It's really sweet. You know, all my life I've never really had the chance to form friendships that last too long. It was such a revolving door and when I came to this place I was afraid that it would be the same. But I'm glad that I met you guys. You've made this place way better than it would have been otherwise. I've never been good at making friends, so if I hadn't met you I'm not sure I would have made any friends, and I'd have to deal with Julia all by myself."

"You're welcome, and we're glad that you've come along," Josh said.

He shared out the food. Troy came down, and Adam came near as well, although he took some food away and continued tending to his flowers, caressing them as though they were a lover. I looked at him a little differently, now that I knew the truth of what had happened. I felt pity that his heart was so big, his only crime was that he had loved someone too fiercely and hadn't known when to stop. I dared not say anything though as I didn't want to embarrass him.

We ate the food. Troy told me about the game and we joked around. Once we'd finished eating we rested on the ground, staring up at the stars. It was endless in its beauty and as I gazed up at the sky it felt as though I was being pulled into infinity.

"It's so beautiful isn't it?" I whispered.

I looked over and saw that Adam tilted his head back, following our gazes. Troy and Josh were either side of me. The moon was full and sensual, and as we spoke quietly it felt as though we were the only people in the world. Troy and Josh agreed with me, and we were comfortable in our silence together. I listened to the rhythm of their breathing, and when I glanced over I saw their chests rise and fall. We were so close and it was so silent that I could almost hear their hearts beating.

After some time, Josh broke the silence.

"Elsa, there's something we wanted to tell you, something about ourselves that might make you feel a little better as in it might make you realize that you're not the only one who has been through a painful experience."

"What's that?" I asked, furrowing my brow.

"I know we told you that we're all friends because we arrived here at the same time, but that's not the entire truth. There's something else we had in common," Troy said, taking up the baton of conversation. He breathed in deeply and I wondered what they were going to say. In the momentary silence, I wondered what it was going to be, but I couldn't think. I glanced over at Adam to see if I could glean any hint from him, but he was just staring into space, seemingly unconcerned about our conversation.

"It's not a big deal and it's nothing to be concerned about, but we're all cancer survivors. We met when we were inducted into an experimental trial and because we had to be monitored it was decided that a traditional education model wasn't suitable for us, so Angel Academy opened up their places. Our chances of survival weren't great, but we all thought we should give it a shot and, thankfully, it worked for all three of us. We've all had our brush with death, as well. I know it's not the same as you losing your parents, but we've all thought about our own mortality."

As soon as he said this, so many things clicked into place. It all seemed to make sense; Josh's earlier mention of something that changed him into a new man, Adam's obsession with death and life...it was all so clear to me and I felt closer to them. I thanked them for telling me and I wondered why they hadn't told me sooner, but they said it was something they didn't like to dwell upon.

"What was the experimental treatment?" I asked. They glanced at each other.

"It was just this new drug," Josh said.

"The chances of it working were slim, but we figured we might as well give it a shot. Otherwise we'd have died and that didn't seem fun at all," Troy said.

"Well, I'm very glad you took it. I can't really imagine the world without you in it," I said. Josh and Troy chuckled, assuming that I was joking, but I wasn't. "I really mean it. I know we haven't known each other for that long, but you've been there for me when I've needed you and I don't know that there's anyone else who would have done this for me. I've always struggled to surround myself with people who could be a family. Part of me has always wanted that, to be a part of something bigger than myself. I thought that...something else in my life might give me that opportunity, but now I don't think it will. I think it's things like this that have that effect. I think it's important to make connections with people and to hold onto them."

As I said this, without meaning to, my hands found Troy's and Josh's. I held them tightly and squeezed. I felt the warmth of their hands and our fingers laced together. It felt right holding them both. I sat up and looked at each of them. Some kind of spell came over us; it was as though I was enchanted by the moon and I was filled with courage from some primal, fey source. Josh and Troy pushed themselves up as well. I was in between the two of them and I turned my gaze from one to the other, letting my gaze linger on their soft, full lips, on the eyes that swam with silver, and I could feel myself being pulled to both of them. My own lips parted and my breath rushed out, warm against my cool lips. Still holding their hands, I leaned into Josh and he leaned back, as though we were drawn together in a dance that had already been performed. My lips pressed against his tenderly and I let out a soft moan. His taste lingered and the heat of his breath wrapped around my cheeks and chin. My heart fluttered inside my chest and goosebumps prickled on my skin. I adjusted my body and turned to lean into Troy, who caught my lips in a more passionate kiss. His lips were firm and hard, and I whimpered. I was left dazed as I was caught between the two men.

I remembered the dream. My ancestor, who also enjoyed the pleasure of more than one lover. It felt right. It felt natural. But it wasn't complete yet.

"Adam," I said in a soft, clear voice that broke the stillness of the night, "come here," I said. It was a gentle command, but a command nonetheless. Adam looked up from his flowers, a profound sadness in his eyes.

"I can't. I'll only hurt you," he said.

"No, you won't. Josh told me what happened before. Your only crime was loving someone who didn't love you back. I'll show you what it's like to be truly intimate with someone," I said.

"It's not right. You don't know-" he protested, his voice trembling with panic.

"I know enough," I said tenderly. "You're safe with us. We'll keep each other safe. There's nothing you need to worry about." I held up my hand, waiting for him to take it. He seemed unsure, but eventually he managed to pull himself away from his flowers and came towards us. Josh and Troy both smiled and welcomed him. He kneeled before me. I wrapped my arms around his shoulders and embraced him tightly, before I kissed him again, this time more deeply than we had kissed before. "It's okay Adam, you can let yourself go. I'll take care of you."

Being with them opened up my heart to a nurturing side of which I had never been aware. I realized then that I had always had a deep need to surround myself with love, and one person would never have been enough, because I wanted to replace the love of a family that I had never had. I looked at the three men and knew I was feeling affection for each of them for different reasons, but there wasn't one I liked more than another. There was no limit to the amount of love I could feel; it swelled and swelled, but it would never burst. This felt right, this felt natural, and if the only message my ancestor had been trying to tell me was that this kind of relationship was possible then the message had been received loud and clear, and I was grateful for her.

Adam sat in front of me. Josh and Troy had their arms around my body, supporting me like pillars. I traded kisses with each of them, moving between one and another, loving the feeling that came with each one, loving the differences between them. I closed my eyes and started playing a game with myself to see if I could tell which one was which. I'm proud to say I got it right every time. Our bodies were pressed so closely together that there was barely any air between us. I felt Troy's hand resting against the small of my back. Josh's played with my hair. Adam held my hands gently and I was cocooned in their love. Everything went unspoken, as though there was a common understanding between us and we didn't have to talk about what the dynamic was. Each of us knew exactly what was happening and it all seemed perfectly natural.

I arched my neck back and offered them my neck, enjoying the feeling of them kissing down the hollow of my throat. I felt a hand groping my breasts and I began to ache in between my thighs. My own hands reached out, exploring their bodies, tugging at their tops, running down their flat stomachs, finding the bulges that throbbed with intense heat. I gasped as I felt their arousal and the heat made the air sizzle. The kisses grew deeper, longer, our tongues danced and tingles spread all over my body. My dress was pulled aside. There was a mouth on my breast, sucking at the hard nipple. A hand ran up my thigh, teasing the soft, burning flesh of my inner thigh, threatening to reach my most intimate area. A grunt was in my ear as someone whispered sweet nothings to me and nibbled my lobe. A smile played on my lips at the tickling feeling, but it was quickly swept away by another kiss. I moaned and whimpered as the men blurred together. They were my boys, and I was filled with a deep need to take care of them, and a desire to enjoy them.

I made them take off their tops, exposing their bodies. They were sexy and muscular, but their skin was surprisingly cool. I was intoxicated by the scent of their bodies and my hands delved down, groping their thighs, tugging at their belts. I moaned as they fumbled with their clasps, eager to expose themselves to me, while I spread my legs and grabbed their wrists, pulling their hands closer towards my burning wetness. I bit my lower lip as they touched my most intimate area and I almost screamed, the feeling was so good. Their fingers curled back and forth inside me, stroking me, getting deeper and deeper with every passing moment. The heat flared through my body as though I had been impaled on a fiery spike. My chest flushed and my mind cracked. My eyes clamped shut and I welcomed the intense sensations coursing through my body, as fast as the wind and as electric as a crackling thunderstorm.

Sweat prickled on my brow in the cool night as the pleasure ran rampant between us. Troy and Josh lowered me back and Adam fell forward, for it had been his hands that had been pleasuring me, and now it turned to his mouth. He buried himself in between my thighs and I was surprised steam or smoke didn't smolder around his mouth for I felt so hot. I clutched his scalp and my body writhed underneath the force of the pleasure, but I couldn't concentrate on him fully because I had two other men. Josh and Troy kissed and caressed me. It felt as though a hundred hands were all over my body, and I loved every minute of it. I wanted them so badly. I wanted more and more. My appetite was caught in a frenzy and I had a thirst that only they could slake. I cried out for their bodies, needing to be with them, to be close to them, needing to feel them inside me. Adam's tongue danced. He was a maestro and he was creating a masterpiece between my legs. Orgasmic energy throbbed and swelled and burst through me like a supernova, crashing wildly again and again as I was seized in a world of delight.

I was all ready to take them one by one inside me, ready to lose my virginity to them, but then suddenly the moment was lost.

"Wait," Josh whispered, his tone harsh and tense. He looked up, as did Troy. They looked towards the building.

"Shit, Elsa, you have to go," Josh said. Adam looked up, his mouth dripping with my wetness. He looked dazed and saw how panicked the other two were.

"They've seen us. If you're caught you're going to be in a world of trouble. Elsa, you have to leave now," Josh hissed. I gathered myself up and fled, running towards the gates through the darkness. The fear laced my desire and although I was disappointed that it had ended so abruptly, I was also delirious and exhilarated at the thought of what would happen the next time. I had broached a new frontier with my three boys and I couldn't wait to see them again. This was the beginning of something special, and I was filled with happiness.

*

I clambered over the wall and made my way home, enjoying the peace of the night. I had no idea how Josh had managed to see anyone coming from the house, but I had to be grateful for his keen senses as he had saved my skin. After what happened with Julia, the last thing I wanted was to be seen on the grounds after curfew, although I didn't know how they were going to explain it away. I had faith in their charm though, and hopefully they would get a rap on the knuckles at most.

As I calmed down I thought about what they had told me; how they had been diagnosed with cancer and had to face their mortality. I wondered what must have been going through their minds, how hopeless life must have felt. The one mercy for my parents was that it had all been over quickly so they had no time to think about what they would be missing out on and lament their fate. I would hate to wither away, and it was fortunate that they had found a treatment that worked. Life was balanced on such strokes of fate, and, hopefully, it was a treatment that could benefit others. There were a lot of questions I wanted to ask them about their illness that didn't seem appropriate at the time. I wondered if they were fully cured, as well, or had just gone into remission. It also explained why Adam had enjoyed such intense feelings for the girl he hurt, as well. If he thought he was terminal he would have wanted to experience love before he died. I hoped that I could give him everything he needed now and that we could all be happy. I knew that I had found something that I had been craving, something that I had needed for a long time. I didn't know until I'd found it though, and I wasn't going to give it up. Part of me was afraid that, like my first kiss with Adam, it would just be a product of a single night, but I had faith that the four of us had made a sacred pact and it would take a strong force to break it.

I wasn't going to tell Arthur. I had a feeling he would disapprove, probably saying that at this crucial stage I should be focusing on my studies and my training as a Slayer so that I could be ready whenever the time came to face the master vampires. I also wanted to keep something that was just mine as well. Not everything in my life had to be touched by the fact that I was a Slayer. This was something that was private and personal, and if Arthur was allowed his secrets, I was too.

*

I returned home feeling good about myself, even though I had neglected my patrol for the evening. I vowed to make up for it the following night though. When I got to the house I was surprised to see that the lights were on. Usually Arthur was asleep by this time, so my hackles rose and I tensed my muscles, ready to defend him if there were any unsavory characters. I peeked into the windows but the curtains were drawn, and while I didn't want to be paranoid I wanted to be cautious. I decided to walk around the back and carefully opened a window. I twisted myself through the small opening and dropped to the floor, arching my feet so that I cushioned the blow and made as little noise as possible. I skulked through the darkness and heard the sound of muffled voices. I wondered if it was a member of the council coming to check up on the two of us. I had heard that they liked their surprise visits, to make sure their watchers and Slayers were obeying protocol. It seemed an odd time of the night to visit, but the council always seemed to keep odd timings.

I walked to the door on tiptoes and pressed my ear closely. I heard two voices, and as I cracked open the door a sliver of light poured through. It only took a few words for me to realize that I recognized the voice. As soon as I did I burst through the door and stormed into the room, my jaw dropping open at the sight of Julia sitting at the table with Arthur. I jabbed a finger in the air.

"What the hell is she doing here?"

# Chapter Thirteen

I couldn't believe that Julia, the Julia, the bane of my existence, was sitting with Arthur in my home. Her eyes narrowed when she saw me, but there was a flicker of her trademark smugness as well. I walked all the way up to the table and looked at Arthur expectantly.

"So, this is the Slayer. I never would have expected it. I'm surprised you didn't use any of your abilities on me," Julia said. I glared at her, but wasn't ready to indulge her in any kind of conversation. Even though we had bonded over tragedy we weren't anywhere near close to calling each other friends and I certainly wasn't ready to have her involved in this secret. My mind was wild with thoughts about how she had arrived here. When I first saw her I thought she might have actually figured it out somehow, but the first thing she said to me discounted that possibility. The only other explanation wasn't something I wanted to consider.

Arthur was calm, as always, and he spoke quietly and softly.

"I assume this is the Julia that you have told me about?" he asked.

I nodded, and was annoyed that he hadn't answered my question. "Why is she here?" I demanded.

Julia was the one who answered.

"It turns out that my mother was a Slayer, and Arthur here was kind enough to get in touch with me and tell me of my destiny. I always knew there was something special about me."

"No," I gasped. Arthur shifted his glance between the two of us and sighed.

"Elsa, come with me, let me speak with you in private." He rose from his seat and nodded towards Julia, before escorting me by the arm to another room.

"This is madness. She can't be a Slayer. She just can't!"

"It's true, she is, and I'm the only watcher in the area. I know this is going to be difficult for you given what you've told me, and I can certainly tell that she's a little...rough around the edges. But for the sake of the cause we must try and get along." I shook my head. I was just about ready to blow my top and tell him everything wrong with that idea, but he continued speaking. "Just think of the positives. You've been complaining that we've been outnumbered. Two Slayers is a much more formidable prospect than one. We might actually be able to take the fight to the vampires as you want, but you'll need to work as a team. Whatever your differences are, you're going to have to put them aside. There are some things that are more important. You know that the fight we're in is bigger than all of us. We don't have control over who becomes a Slayer, all we can do is help guide them. It's my job, and it's yours too. You can show her everything she needs to know. As you said, it's better to learn from a Slayer."

"You want me to teach her?"

"Take her out on patrol. Show her what she needs to do. When she's ready we can take on the vampires and take the fight to them. This might be exactly what we needed. I don't think anything happens by accident. It's fortunate that she was over here instead of in Europe with her family, although some Slayers do end up sending their children away in case danger befalls them. I imagine that's what her mother did." His tone turned gentler. "Remember how confusing a time this was when you discovered your abilities. It's all new to her and she's going to need help to adjust. She deserves our compassion."

I huffed, knowing that he was right. I would have given anything to have someone to talk to when I first discovered my abilities. Having Arthur there was a help, but there were some things he simply didn't understand. I breathed deeply and tried to calm myself, getting ready for the moment when I had to explain to Julia all the nuances of being a Slayer.

"Are you ready to go back in there?" Arthur asked. "I've explained the history to her and the importance of this fight we're in. She seems to be quite confident that she can handle herself."

"I'm sure she is," I said through gritted teeth, but I nodded and entered the room to talk to her.

"There is something else," he added. "Julia here is descended from the very first Slayer."

I rolled my eyes. Of course she is, I thought. It wouldn't be Julia without her having some kind of special, sacred link that put her above anyone else. I had to remind myself of what she was going through, but when I returned to the room and saw her sitting in the chair as though she owned the place it was difficult for me to reconcile this Julia with the one I'd spent time with in her room, the one who was vulnerable and fragile.

"So, you've been keeping secrets?" she teased, with an arched eyebrow.

"Yes, and you have to keep this secret too. No telling Angelica and the others," I replied. Julia waved her hand dismissively.

"Just tell me what I can do," she asked. I sighed and pinched the bridge of my nose. I looked over to Arthur, who gave me an encouraging nod. All I wanted to do was swim in the memories of the evening, to lose myself in thoughts of lust and pleasure and relive the moments where my three boys had given themselves to me, but instead I was stuck training Julia.

"You can kill vampires. We have heightened senses, agility, strength, and stamina. Our duty is to guard the world against evil and protect the innocent," I said.

"And how is that going?"

I glanced at Arthur, but didn't reply. I didn't want Julia to get the sense that I was a failure. She already had an air of superiority about her. The last thing I wanted was to feed that.

Arthur and I spent the next couple of hours telling her about the different types of vampire and how they could be killed. We showed her the different types of weapons in her arsenal, and talked a little bit about the mythology behind the Slayers. I had heard it all before, but it was interesting to hear it again as Arthur became passionate. It was easy to think of him as a tired old man who was only interested in his books, but he had given his life to this cause when he didn't need to. People like Julia and I didn't have a choice. We were born into the bloodlines and given the blessing of the Slayer, but Arthur volunteered and took it upon himself to educate and guide Slayers into the world. It was easy to forget just how much he had given up in life to help me.

Julia listened inattentively. She didn't seem too bothered about the whole thing and I was surprised, because when I had learned about all this stuff it had been mind-blowing. It was as though a cloak had been lifted from the world and I was given a new perspective on everything. Seeing the truth filled me with wonder, and I knew I would never be the same again, but Julia checked her nails and didn't seem bothered at all.

The dawn sun rose and since it was the weekend we didn't have any classes at the academy, which was good and bad. I was thankful I didn't have to spend more time with Julia at the academy, but I was disappointed I couldn't see Adam, Josh, and Troy. I wanted to talk to them about the previous night and where we went from here. But I had my own duties to perform and Julia needed training, so we arranged for her to come back that night and train with us. As she left I turned to Arthur and groaned.

"I don't think you realize exactly how much trouble we're in for," I said.

His eyes twinkled as he looked back at me. "If I can handle training you, I can handle training anyone," he said. I shook my head because his confidence was misplaced. There was no way I was as difficult as Julia.

*

I rested during the day and caught up on schoolwork, although I found it almost impossible to concentrate on anything other than the boys. A smile played upon my lips constantly as my thoughts shifted between each of them, and more than once I squirmed when I thought about the sensations they had caused in my body. I never knew it was possible to feel such intense things. It made me realize that my brief foray into love, the stolen kiss from Michael, had barely hinted at what was truly possible. I was glad that it was something I could keep to myself. I liked having something personal and hidden, and I couldn't wait to see them again. I just hoped they didn't get into too much trouble because of it.

Julia returned and was eager to get out on the streets and hunt vampires. She was restless as we went through all her weapons again, even though we told her she needed to know how to use them for her own good. She was equipped with the usual items and seemed proud to wear them. Then, we went out into the streets and hunted vampires.

"This is amazing," she said as we went outside. "But how do you handle living with him? He seems so strict."

"He's not so bad, he just likes things to be a certain way."

"I can't believe you kept this hidden from us. I guess that's why you're not staying in the dorms?"

"That's right. Julia, you know I was being serious when I told you that you can't tell anyone about this, right? This isn't some kind of game. This is real and we have to protect the secret so that we can keep Slayers safe."

Julia gave me a patronizing look. "Elsa, don't be such a spoilsport. Look, the fact is that I'm not as naïve as you think I am. You see, when I suddenly started feeling different I realized something. All this time I thought my Mom hated me, that my parents just wanted to forget about me, but I know now that they only wanted to protect me and that really they gave me something special. Mom told me stories when I was younger. I thought they were just little fairytales at first, but when I saw Arthur and he explained things to me it all made sense. I realized the stories weren't just stories at all, but she was preparing me for the future! So yes, I'll keep it a secret, because my Mom obviously thought it was important, but I'm not going to be grim about this destiny."

I have to admit I was a little envious that she had managed to get some closure with her parents and learn that they had sent her away for her own protection. It gave her a connection with them that I never had with my own parents, and the common bond that existed between myself and Julia weakened.

"I used to think she was making things up about Slayers and vampires," Julia continued. "I never gave it much thought when I was growing up, but it's all starting to come back to me now. Mom always told me that things weren't as they seemed. She said there was a true story, one that they didn't tell you, about the very beginning."

"What kind of story?" I asked.

"Slayers and vampires have existed from the very beginning and it's all tied up with Christianity. Think about the Garden of Eden. The serpent that came to Eve...it wasn't a serpent at all. It was a vampire trying to seduce her away. Eve was the first Slayer. She was tempted, but when she ate the apple she saw the truth and she killed the vampire. It's always been something that's existed in the world, but Mom said that people like to hide the truth because it would change everything if they knew. I never actually thought there was any truth to it."

I don't know if Julia realized what a bombshell she had just dropped. I stared at her, agape, wondering if this was actually true or if her Mom had just lied and made this all up, because if we were descended from the first woman...it meant that this wasn't some magical thing at all, and it also meant that Slayers and vampires were caught in an endless dance.

"So what kind of things do we do anyway? Where are the vampires?" she asked, looking around as we walked through the dark streets of the city. I told her to keep her voice down because we didn't want anyone to overhear us, but she didn't seem bothered.

"It's not like they'd believe us anyway," she said. I just shook my head. It wasn't long before we came across our first vampire. I found the tracks and we followed them to an old warehouse. The shadows danced and the only light was from the moon. It poured in through the skylight and it was clear that the vampire had made this his lair. It was perfect really; close enough to the city that the creature could make it there without too much trouble, but far enough away that it could retreat during the day and remain undisturbed. I put my finger to my lips and strained my ears, listening for the tiniest sound. Julia wasn't being careful at all. She didn't pay attention and walked right into the middle of the room, pulling her stake out and calling for the vampire. I hissed at her to come back.

"Don't worry, we're Slayers, right? We're made to kill them," she turned and called towards me, but then the shadows moved and a feral vampire leaped out of the darkness with its fangs and claws bared. Julia shrieked as she turned and saw it. She raised her hands and stabbed wildly with her stake, but she only hit air. The vampire hissed and writhed, swiping at her flailing arms and it was only pure chance that she didn't fall victim to its attacks. I ran forward, the wooden boards creaking under my feet, and threw myself through the air. The vampire turned to face me but I ducked under its claws and jabbed my stake up into its heart. There was a momentary look of panic on its face before it turned to dust.

Julia was panting.

"What the hell do you think you're doing? You could have been killed on your first night! This isn't a game Julia. You have to pay attention to what you're doing. I'm not going to go back to Arthur and tell him that you died during the first night. And these are feral vampires. What hope do you have when we eventually go up against the masters? This isn't Angel Academy. You don't have the run of the school and nobody out here is going to bend to your will like they do at school. You're not in control here and you can't just treat everything like it doesn't matter, because if you make a mistake out here then you're dead."

Julia was on her knees, still trembling. Part of me hated being harsh with her when she had just been through something traumatic, but another part of me figured it was the only way she was going to learn. She had to know how serious this was. She looked up at me and I think she understood that while we were out of the academy I was the one in control. I was the one who knew what she was doing, and I had just saved Julia's life.

"I would have died if it wasn't for you," she said meekly. I held out my hand and helped her up, after glancing around to make sure there weren't any other vampires lurking nearby.

"We all have to learn at some point," I said. "This is a dangerous world. The academy is easy. Out here...one mistake can end everything. I've come close a few times myself."

"You made it look so easy."

"I've just been at this longer than you have. It's something you'll pick up as we go along. You'll get the hang of it, and when you're ready we'll be able to take on the masters. It's rare for two Slayers to be in such close proximity as us, so we have something of an advantage. I've been trying to think of a way to coax them out, but it wasn't possible with just me. With two of us we might be able to set a trap."

"I hate to think there's something worse than them," she shuddered.

"They're just feral. They're dangerous, but they don't plan ahead. They just live by instinct. We need to get to the ones who are behind all this, if we have any hope of stopping the spread of vampires."

"Do you think they can be stopped?"

"I'm assuming so. It might take some time, but that's why we're here after all, isn't it? What's the point of Slayers if vampires can't be brought under control?"

"I just mean, like...Mom always told me that there should be balance in the world and I think she might have been talking about Slayers and vampires. If what she said was true and that balance has been there ever since the beginning, maybe it's never going to be possible to end things. To be honest, the way she spoke about things she never even made being a vampire sound that bad..."

"What are you talking about?" I asked, looking at Julia incredulously. We had moved outside again and were by the docks. The water at the edge of the city undulated like black glass. The moon reflected off it, and in the distance thin grey clouds floated across the horizon. Our footsteps echoed against the stone ground.

"Well, if you think about it, it's not really the end of the world is it. Not if you're a proper vampire I mean, not one of those...things," she screwed up her face in disgust.

"You mean apart from losing your soul and having to feed on people to survive?"

"Do you really lose your soul though? What is a soul anyway? Are you any different now that you're a Slayer? Maybe it's the same thing. But you get to live forever, that seems like it would be worth a lot to me."

"I don't know, I think it might get a little boring."

"If our parents were vampires they wouldn't have had to die..." Julia said in a quiet voice. I was quiet too. I didn't want to think about what she was saying, because I was afraid it would make too much sense. It was easier for me to believe that vampires were evil and humans were good. That's what Arthur had taught me. That was the battle that had raged through the centuries, and that was the fight I was going to fight.

"Come on," I said, "let's see you have another go, and this time be careful and do exactly what I tell you."

We tracked another vampire. This time Julia was more cautious. I told her exactly what to do before the fight and, aside from a few missteps, she managed to kill her first vampire. We gave each other a high five and she thanked me for helping her out. We didn't talk about the ramifications of vampirism or theories about the origins of the Slayers. It made my head hurt. But I considered the night to be a success and when we departed she actually thanked me. Julia! I never thought I'd see humility from her.

*

"So, how was your first night of training?" Arthur asked after Julia had left. She looked with derision at the books he had prepared for her. I had had to read the same things, and I was amused that she had to go through them as well. I exhaled deeply when she left and tension released from my body.

"It was okay for the most part. She was trouble at first, but when she almost died she started to see things my way."

"Sometimes it takes a shock to the system for people to gain clarity. Was she alright after that?"

"Yes, she was," I said. "She did say a few things that I found surprising though."

"Oh?" Arthur asked with an inquiring gaze. I told him about her opinions about vampires and the stories her mother had told her. Arthur furrowed his brow. "This is rather troubling."

"Is it?"

"Of course," he flashed his eyes towards me, and I could see the whites of them. "The lure of vampirism does take hold of some people and they become blinded by the evil. It's all too easy to let ourselves be fooled into thinking that they're not evil, but they are, and we must remain vigilant. This...this myth is something I have heard before. It's a story misguided people tell themselves to try and understand the world better. It's a dangerous way of thinking and you must remain vigilant. Keep a close eye on her. We cannot let a Slayer turn to their side. The consequences would be disastrous."

"I don't think she's thinking anything like that," I said. "But what would you have me do if she does end up sympathizing with the enemy?"

Arthur's shoulders sagged and he looked as though he had aged a hundred years in a matter of moments. "She must be stopped," he said simply, but I felt the ominous nature of his words, and I wondered how many other Slayers had gone down that path, and how many had been stopped. It suddenly made me wonder about my own position as a Slayer and how I could be under threat too. I thought back to that conversation I had overheard and wondered if the council had ever thought about stopping me, or what it would take for them to try. Tension ran through my body and I didn't know what else to think. Was there always a danger of new Slayers walking down the wrong path?

"Have you had any more dreams lately?" Arthur asked, as if the thought had just occurred to him.

"No, I haven't," I replied. I was telling the truth, but at this point I wasn't sure I would tell him, even if I had. I thought I had gotten the message I needed from my mysterious ancestor, but was sure that there was something else my aunt hadn't told me. I hadn't had any other dreams from her though and the longer she was silent the more I wondered if that one single dream had just been a product of my own mind rather than an echo of a memory.

# Chapter Fourteen

I returned to the Academy on Monday with excitement. I couldn't wait to see Josh and the others again. I got there early to try and catch them between breakfast and the start of classes. But it wasn't them who I saw first; it was Julia, who was flanked by the usual suspects. We passed each other and exchanged a knowing glance, although breath caught in my throat because I wondered if she was going to go against her word and reveal our secrets to her friends. Angelica looked at me with a scornful expression and sneered. She made a comment as we passed, but before I could bite back with an insult of my own Julia interceded.

"Leave her Angelica. She's off limits now," Julia said. Angelica's face reddened as if she couldn't believe it, but she obeyed Julia's wishes without question. I assumed it was thanks for saving Julia's life and I was glad to see that finally something had changed. Given everything that had happened with the boys on Friday I had the feeling that things were changing for the better and I couldn't wait for the rest of my life to begin. I hadn't been convinced of the advantages of the academy during my first couple of weeks, but I was beginning to adjust to the life and it was getting better at every moment.

I searched the dining hall for signs of the boys, but I didn't catch sight of any of them. I thought about going to the dorms but then I saw what I thought was Josh near the entrance. I went back that way and saw him coming out of Mrs. Thorpe's office. I ran up to him with an excited smile on my face. We were near the entrance of the academy and the sun shone outside. People were coming back from the weekend so there were cars moving outside the entrance, some of them driving off rather abruptly, as parents seemed eager to get away from their children.

I tugged at Josh's arm, feeling as though flinging my arms around him in an emphatic embrace was a little too much for so early in the morning. When he turned to face me, I knew that something was wrong. His heart was stone and his eyes had lost some of their light. He looked as though he hadn't slept since I'd last seen him. He was so weak and vulnerable.

"What's wrong?" I asked.

He went to turn away without saying anything, I had no idea why. I pulled him back. "Josh, talk to me."

"I'm sorry Elsa," he said in a rasp, "but I can't."

"What? Why not? What about Friday?"

"That was...that was a mistake. I'm sorry. We shouldn't have done that. We all got a little carried away I think. It's not right. I wish things could be different but they aren't."

His words stabbed me, each one was like a dagger in my heart. "What are you talking about?" I asked in disbelief. "We all enjoyed it. You can't mean this. What do the others think?"

"They feel the same. It's...it's not us Elsa, and it's not you either it's just that some things can't happen. I see that now and I'm sorry that we let it get this far."

I couldn't believe what I was hearing. It seemed as though it wasn't really Josh speaking at all, as though someone else was speaking through him, but I didn't know if that was just my own wishful thinking or not. The world seemed to shimmer and lurch around me. I felt as though I was going to lose my balance.

"I think it's better that we stop seeing each other. All of us," he added. That broke my soul. Everything was being ripped away from me and I couldn't stop any of it. My mind was frantic, trying to figure out what had gone wrong, but I just couldn't think of any of it. My eyes darted from side to side and I tried to make sense of it all, but I just couldn't. The boys were the only thing that made this place palatable and without them I was back to being the lonely unwanted girl from the orphanage. Was I never meant to be happy? How was I going to continue the Slayer bloodline if I couldn't even fall in love right?

Adam warned me about this as well. He said that he had hurt someone in the past and now I had been hurt too. I wanted to get out of there. I needed fresh air. There were so many things I wanted to say to Josh. I wanted to scream, and shout, and rant, and tear out my hair, but everything was jumbled and my lips felt locked together. There was a lump in my throat and a sick twisting in my stomach. I staggered away from him and my name on his lips became a whisper. I went towards the light. My mind was hazy and dazed. All I could think was about how good I had felt with them, and how I would never feel that way again.

I stepped out of the entrance and was blinded by the sun. I was so lost in my own fractured soul that I didn't hear the roar of an engine or feel the tremor of the car that wanted to speed away. I looked around, panicked but it was too late. Even my superior Slayer agility wasn't quick enough to save me.

But Josh was.

He leapt out at me and dragged me away. The car swerved. Tires screeched. It narrowly missed me and the horn blared. Gravel crunched loudly as it sped away past the fountain and disappeared into the distance. Breath rushed out of me as I looked down to check myself for injuries, surprised that I was unharmed. I heard Josh wince beside me. At first I assumed he had been wounded by the car, but that didn't make any sense because he hadn't been anywhere near it. The only way the car could have hurt him was if it had rammed through me first. But Josh cried out in pain and he was almost smoldering. I reached out for him, not understanding how he was in such anguish. He had turned away, but as I moved around I saw that his face was mottled, scarred, and withered. I shook my head, astonished and distraught, because I had seen these types of wounds before. It couldn't be true, but as thoughts rampaged through my mind I realized that they must have been. It made sense now why Adam had the curtains drawn in his room and why he only liked going out at night. Josh didn't like going to the gardens because of his allergies, it was because of something else entirely.

It was because they were vampires.

I took one look at Josh's wounds and tore myself away from him. I sprinted in the opposite direction, not caring about classes or anything else. The last thing I heard was him calling after me, but he didn't chase me. He couldn't. He had to get back to the shadows, back where he belonged.

*

I ran until I could run no longer. I ran until I was out of breath and my limbs were on fire. Nothing made any sense anymore. My world had been destroyed and I didn't know how to cope. All this time I had been falling in love with vampires and I hadn't even realized it. I should have, especially given how in the dream the faces of the vampires had been replaced with those of my boys, but I thought it was all just a metaphor. I worried that they were the masters, that I would have to kill them. I felt like throwing up and I wasn't sure how I was going to tell Arthur about this, or Julia. Were there more vampires at the academy? So many questions ran through my mind, but the heart of the matter was that I didn't think I could kill the boys. I didn't know if I had it in me and yet I knew I would have to because that was my duty as a Slayer.

I was so frustrated because I felt that finally I had something in my life that wasn't touched by the fact that I was a Slayer, yet when it had come down to it, it bled into every area of my life. I wondered if I would ever be happy. I didn't know how I was going to go back to the academy after this and I ended up wandering around for hours. I watched the sun set and I was completely lost in my own mind. I would usually have gone to Arthur for guidance, but I was worried that cavorting with vampires would go against the Slayer code and I would be targeted for termination by the council. I didn't even feel like going on patrol for vampires. I didn't want to do anything other than sort out the mess in my own mind.

I wandered the streets aimlessly, walking like a vagrant, with no purpose and no direction. I almost bumped into people as I staggered through the streets and once the shadows had set I felt more like I was at home. The air was cool and the streets became emptier. I wanted to feel as though I was the only person in the world. It was easier being alone. You didn't have to worry about anyone hurting you, and I started to regress to the girl I used to be, the one who pushed everyone away without a second thought. My heart dried up into a cold stone and I vowed I would never let myself get carried away with my emotions again.

After walking for, I don't know how long, I heard footsteps behind me. I turned around, ready to fight. But my fists dropped when I saw it was Josh. His wounds had healed. I tensed and looked around to see if there were any other vampires with him but he was alone. He held up his hands and looked apologetic. I was tempted to walk away but as soon as I saw him again my heart melted and I felt a tug at my emotions. It was difficult to stuff emotions back into a heart, once they had been released.

"What are you doing here?" I asked.

"I wanted to explain about what happened earlier."

"I don't need your explanations. What are you going to tell me, that it's allergies again?"

"I'm sorry," he said, letting his head dip. "It made sense at the time. I needed to tell you something, and I thought you'd never believed the truth. But when you saw me today...you know, don't you?"

"That you're a vampire?"

He seemed visibly relieved when I mentioned the word. "I'm sorry for not telling you. I'm sure you can understand why. It's how I tracked you here. You covered a lot of distance today."

"You put yourself at risk when you saved me," I said, thinking about how he thrust himself into the light without any hesitation, to pull me out of the way of the moving car. Despite everything else I at least owed him my gratitude for that.

"I couldn't let any harm come to you. I care for you, deeply."

"That's not what you said earlier," I snapped. Part of me was relieved to see him, but another part of me was still angry and just wanted to have a go at him for hiding this from me. He looked shocked at the vehemence of my words and actually seemed wounded.

"It wasn't fair. I know. I just...it's a complicated situation. You remember when I said that I wanted to understand myself before I became involved with someone else? This is why."

"When you talked about a transformation I assumed that you were talking about the cancer. You were talking about this, weren't you?" I asked. He nodded. "Was any of it true? Were you lying about the cancer as well?"

"No, I would never lie about that. Look, come with me and we can talk more," he said, gesturing to a park nearby. It could have been a trap, but I didn't feel threatened by him, so I nodded and followed him into the park. In the day this place would have been filled with people strolling around, running, playing with their dogs and having picnics. At night it was the complete opposite. The lampposts dotted the path with light. We found a bench and sat down. There was distance between us. I still hadn't told him I was a Slayer yet. I wasn't sure how to broach that particular subject, but I knew I couldn't avoid it forever.

"How did you know I was a vampire?" he asked as we sat down.

"I think you owe me answers first," I said. "Tell me how you became vampires."

He placed his hands on his thighs and leaned forward, taking a few moments to compose himself. He stared into space and spoke slowly, as though he wasn't accustomed to telling this story.

"We weren't lying about the cancer. We were all in the same ward, dying a slow death. There seemed to be no hope for us and then one day we were told that there was a special treatment. We were all surprised because we thought that we'd exhausted all our options, and by this point we were willing to try anything. We met with...a representative and they explained everything. I was surprised at how open they were, actually, but they said that nobody would believe us if we told the truth, and that if we didn't accept the treatment we wouldn't be able to tell anyone anyway. It was harsh, but true. All we had to do was give ourselves, become vampires, and we'd be cured. We would have a place at the academy for as long as we wanted and we would be alive. I don't think any of us hesitated for long. Maybe Adam was the longest. It seemed like a no brainer. But I didn't realize how much we were giving up. Ever since then, I have to wonder if I'm the same person I was. If I really saved myself or just brought some new life into existence? When we changed I'd forgotten what it was like to feel healthy all the time. Sure, we couldn't go out in sunlight and things like that, but at least we were alive. We celebrated when we lived past the point at which we had been told we were going to die. We were given a chance at a new life, and I know you probably think I'm a monster, but are you going to tell me that you wouldn't have chosen the same fate?"

I listened to what he had to say and couldn't say that I wouldn't have. It was similar to the conversation I'd had with Julia. If they hadn't been turned into vampires, Josh and the others would have died. I'd always thought of vampirism as an evil thing, but in this way it could save people as well.

"I don't know," I said. "But surely it's evil? What do you do when you need to feed?" I asked, almost afraid of the answer.

"We don't feed on people if that's what you're afraid of. We have animal blood. I'd never want to turn anyone or anything like that. We just wanted to live, that's all, and when we met you we realized that something special had happened."

"Wait..." I asked, suddenly thinking of something, "when Adam told me that he'd hurt someone he cared about...?"

I trailed off. Josh licked his lips. "When we first shifted it was different. We weren't used to how things worked. There was a girl in the ward with us. She and Adam were close, but she didn't want the same treatment. She had made peace with the fact that she was going to die and wasn't going to fight what she saw as the plan for her. Adam couldn't understand how anyone could give up on life that easily and she explained it by saying that every flower had to wilt. That's why he's so interested in botany, because she was. He was convinced that if she could just see what was happening with us she would change her mind and they could be together forever, so after we had been transformed he went back to see her and he told her what had happened. He told her everything, but it didn't go as he planned. She was terrified and screamed. He tried to hold her down, but he was stronger than before and he didn't realize it yet. Bones cracked and she just managed to push him away. She told him never to come near her again. He never got to say goodbye."

"That's awful," I said, my heart broke for Adam all over again.

"Yes. We decided that it would be better if we didn't involve ourselves with normal people again, not in that way, not with anyone who wouldn't understand. You seemed different though. I'm not even sure why."

"So then why did you change your mind? Why did you pull away today? Friday was amazing. I thought we all had a good time and it was going to be the beginning of something new. I was really looking forward to coming back here and talking about where the four of us were going. Instead I was told the complete opposite. What happened over the weekend?"

Josh sighed. "I wouldn't ordinarily tell you this, but you're special and you deserve an explanation. The ones who turned us...they forbade us from entering into a union with you. It breaks their rules and as much as I'd love to turn away from them I can't. None of us can. I'm sorry. I know you probably don't understand how it works and I hope you can appreciate me being honest with you."

"I do," I said, thoughts churning around in my mind. "But when you say that your master wouldn't let you? Does that mean they're at the academy too?"

"I'm not supposed to talk about it," he said. "I'm not supposed to talk about this at all."

"Please Josh. I think I deserve to know if people in the academy are vampires. I already know it has to be someone because you never go anywhere else, and I'm not going to feel safe if I have to be suspicious of everyone. I won't tell anyone. I promise," I lied. Despite my personal feelings for Josh I had to seize this opportunity. These people had to be the masters in the area, the ones I had been longing to find, and now I finally had a way to get close to them.

"It's the three of them. Mrs. Thorpe, Mr. Griff, and Mr. Hanon. That's why the academy is so different from every other school. It can afford to be. They don't turn everyone, and I'll always be grateful to them because they saved me. I hope you can understand that."

"You should leave them," I said.

"I can't. It's too hard. I owe them my life."

"But what kind of life are you living now? You don't get to do what you want. You talked to me about your dreams and ambitions. What did you want to be before you were changed?"

"I wanted to be a writer. I wanted to travel the world and write about everything I experienced."

"Then do that! Leave. You were given a chance at life, it's not fair that it's been taken from you. Are you planning to stay at the Academy forever?"

Josh fell silent.

"You can make all the excuses for them that you want, but when it comes down to it, if they're not willing to give you your freedom, then how much have they really saved you? It's not fair to any of you to keep you like this. They're just collecting you Josh. You need to fight back."

Josh's face hardened. He folded his arms across his chest defensively.

"You don't understand," he said. I could tell that I wasn't going to get through to him now. Arthur had told me all about this, how vampires manipulated people they turned and made them dependent. It wasn't Josh's fault, or any of the others. If I was terminally ill I'd probably cling to whatever thread was dangled in front of me to stay alive, as well, and although they were vampires they weren't evil. But it didn't mean that their masters weren't. I knew I had sensed a strange feeling when I had been interviewed with them, and I was annoyed with myself that I had been so close to them, without being aware of them. But that was how good these experienced vampires were and it showed exactly what the Slayers were up against.

"Just think about it, please." I said, hoping that somehow they would be able to break free of the programming. I didn't want to have to fight them if they came to the defense of their masters.

"So how did you know that I was a vampire?" Josh asked. "I've told you everything. You can at least tell me that. It shouldn't have been that obvious."

This was the moment of truth. I knew that telling him I was a Slayer might make him warn his masters, but I couldn't lie to him. He had saved me at risk to himself, and he had told me the truth. I couldn't see him as the enemy even though he was a vampire. I still cared for him deeply, and I felt an intense flush by being near him. Surprisingly, learning that I'd enjoyed an erotic and sensual experience with a vampire didn't scare me and I did start to wonder if there weren't more shades of grey to life than I had previously imagined.

"I want you to keep this a secret Josh. I'm a Slayer."

His face was pale already, but as I mentioned that word his flesh whitened even more and he backed away.

"No..."

"I'm not going to hurt you, but I am going to have to move against your masters. Are you going to warn them? I need to know now."

Josh looked confused. "I'll...I'll have to talk about it with the others," he said. I could tell by the tone of his voice that he was going to though. If he couldn't break free from them to live his life then he wasn't going to stop himself from warning them. I rose from the bench and tried to think of something else to say, but nothing seemed appropriate. I left him there, wondering if we would ever be able to breech the distance between us.

# Chapter Fifteen

I raced home, knowing there was only limited time to catch the masters unaware before Josh warned them. He seemed so shocked I didn't think he was going to get back to the academy quickly, and I moved as swiftly as I could. I thought about the night we had shared together and realized now that it must have been one of their masters who had interrupted us and forced them to tell me to flee. I couldn't imagine the meeting then, them being scolded and told that being with me was forbidden. They had been held down for so long, shackled by their gratitude for their lives, and all I wanted to do was free them.

Arthur was with Julia. She had started to spend her nights with us to complete her training, and like me she had found it easy to sneak in and out of the academy at night. Arthur saw how panicked I was and I didn't wait for either of them to speak before I told them the news.

"I know where the masters are. They're at the academy. The heads," I said, and relayed the names.

"No way!" Julia said.

"How did you learn this information?" Arthur asked, concern creeping into his voice.

"It doesn't matter how I learned it. What matters is that they're there, and they're so close. We have to go and confront them now," I said.

"You knew today, didn't you? I wondered why you weren't around," Julia said.

Arthur pondered my words.

"No, we must be patient. You might be ready to face them, but Julia certainly isn't. If there's more than one this could be more trouble. I might have to get in touch with the council and get them to send some help. This would be a great coup though. You have done good work Elsa," he said.

"No, you don't understand. We have to go now because they know we're coming," I said. I hated having to tell them that Josh and the others are vampires, but I knew I shouldn't keep it from them.

"How do they know? Did you speak with them?" Arthur asked.

"No I...there's another vampire there. Some boys. They were turned, but they aren't evil. They had cancer and they were offered a treatment to save their lives. They took it. One of them told me about it," I said. Julia gave me a knowing smirk, because she knew exactly which boys I referred to.

Arthur narrowed his eyes at me.

"I'm surprised to hear you talk like that Elsa. You know as well as I do that when someone is turned into a vampire their souls are taken. They're not the same people as they were before. Evil takes root in them and it spreads through them like thorns. We cannot allow evil to spread with such wild abandon. Any vampire is a master waiting to happen. If they have been turned fully then they are being groomed and they will spread the evil and take over their own area of the land. I wouldn't be surprised if these vampires are trying to put people in positions of authority, to educate a select few when they're young and elevate them into power. I will have to go through the records of this academy and see how long this has been going on, but it's good that we found this out now. We can stop it before it goes any further. If what you say is true and time is of the essence then you must go, but please, be careful. Both of you," he said.

I nodded and went up to my room to get ready, gathering all my Slayer equipment. When I returned downstairs Julia was ready to go with me and we left Arthur behind. He seemed fretful and went straight to his study, where he would presumably call the council and tell them of what I had learned.

*

"Julia, no matter what happens tonight I don't want anything to happen to Josh, Adam, or Troy," I said.

"And I thought you believed that every vampire was evil?" she taunted.

"Let's just take care of the masters, okay?" I said tersely. I wasn't in the mood for her teasing. I was just as worried for Josh as I was for myself. I didn't think his masters would take the fact that he had revealed their truth to me lightly. We made our way to the academy. I looked for any sign of Josh, but he was nowhere to be seen. I motioned for Julia to be quiet. We crept past the fountain. Now that I knew this was the home of vampires it had an entirely different feeling. My skin prickled with tension and my eyes darted about, trying to sense any sign of activity.

"Where are they?" Julia whispered.

"Probably inside," I said. We made our way to the door and slipped inside. The lights had been dimmed to a faint glow and a hush had settled over the place. I assumed they were in their rooms, so I signaled for Julia to head towards the stairs, but just as I did we heard footsteps. Mrs. Thorpe emerged from the office where I had been interviewed.

"We've been expecting you. Come this way," she said, gesturing towards the office. Julia glanced at me. Thankfully she seemed to be willing to let me take the lead. I thought there was no choice but to follow her. We walked into the office and saw the three of them sitting at the desk, just as they had been when I had arrived for my interview. Julia and I remained standing. My hand hovered near my precious stake.

"It's taken you quite a while to find us. I'm a little disappointed. I see the standard of Slayers is slipping," Mr. Hanon said. Mr. Griff just stared at us.

"You mean you knew? All this time?" I asked.

Mr. Griff wore a thin smile. There was malevolence in his eyes. "Of course we did. Do you think anything here happens without us knowing? We have taken measures to protect us against your kind. We try to encourage a safe place for the bloodlines. You'll find that a lot of girls here are potential Slayers. Why do you think we kept you around in spite of all your misdemeanors?" his gaze shifted to Julia, who looked dumbfounded and chastened. I had always been warned that master vampires were patient and cunning, but to see it for myself gave me chills.

"It's so nice of you to come to us instead of us coming to you. We have been expecting a showdown for a while, and it's been a while since we've encountered a Slayer," Mr. Hanon said.

"Indeed. Two at once is a rarity. It's quite the boon for us. We're going to be able to brag about this for a while," Mrs. Thorpe said.

"We're here to stop you," I said, hoping that my defiant tone wouldn't betray the fear I was feeling. Just facing one master vampire was daunting enough, let alone three. The three masters chuckled to each other.

"I think your confidence is misplaced. And why would you want to stop us when what we're doing is benefitting humanity?" Mr. Griff said.

"What, by saving people from cancer?" I said.

"I see that the boys couldn't keep their mouths shut," Mrs. Thorpe scowled.

"We save everyone. And we aim to provide them with the skills needed to make this world a better place. Being a vampire gives you a certain perspective about the world that is severely lacking from you regular humans. We take a longer view of things, and surely you can't dispute the fact that humans have made a hash of this planet. All we want is for people to be in a position where they can have a positive influence," Mr. Griff said.

"To push your own agenda you mean. You can't seriously expect me to believe that you want the best for this world. Sure, you might save a few people from cancer, but you don't allow them to have any freedom.

And I've seen all the feral vampires you spread through the city," I said. "You can't tell me they benefit anyone."

"Everything serves their purpose. They serve a form of control. We vampires are an endangered species on the planet. We have to conserve our position and try to keep the human population in check. It's a game of checks and balances," Mr. Hanon said.

"It is, and we're here to keep the balance on the side of the humans. We're not going to let you get away with this. We're Slayers, and we're here to stop you."

I whisked out my stake and held it aloft, gripping it tightly in my hand. Julia copied my gesture, although we weren't in harmony at all. The three vampires seemed amused and grinned at us.

"I was so hoping it would come to this," Mr. Griff said dryly. He rose and opened up his arms. The other two rose as well, and began to move around the table. I moved closer to Julia. We turned our backs to each other and wielded our stakes. In my other hand I pulled out my flask of holy water and popped the lid, throwing it around the room. It hissed as it hit their flesh, but they didn't seem too perturbed by it. Smoke smoldered off their clothes and the room was filled with the smell of brimstone. These master vampires had better resistances than the feral kind. If I had soaked those vampires with holy water they would have shrieked and melted. Despite the holy water not being effective we still had our stakes, and every vampire was vulnerable to these no matter how old and ancient they were. Given Julia's insistence that the Slayers and vampires had been descended from the Garden of Eden I did wonder if the first stake had been from a tree in the Garden of Eden, perhaps it had been a branch from the tree of knowledge. It was only a stray thought that passed through my mind though, because I had to focus on the matter at hand.

Mrs. Thorpe was nearest me, and Mr. Hanon took Julia's side. Mr. Griff loomed over us like a dark shadow. He cackled and I braced myself for combat, unsure if I could win.

"Good luck," I muttered under my breath. Julia thanked me and then suddenly Mrs. Thorpe moved with alarming speed. She rushed forward and her eyes were wild. Her jaws opened and I saw monstrous fangs emerge from her gums, ready to sink into my flesh. Her hands were more like claws as they came around my arms, trying to push me away. I swept my body to the left and kicked out at her leg, trying to unbalance her, but it didn't seem to have any effect. I brought the stake down against her shoulder. It was nowhere near her heart, but I wanted to make her hurt anyway in the hope that it would at least give me some respite. I brought the stake down with all my might, but she twisted her hand and caught my wrist. Her nails dug into my skin and my hand trembled. I gasped in agony. I jabbed my free hand into her stomach and pushed forward, sending her across the table. She landed with a crash and I screamed. She had drawn blood and all the vampires licked their lips at me. I clasped my injured wrist. I felt weak, and I had to change the stake to my other hand.

I was about to press my advantage when I heard a yelp. Julia was being driven back by Mr. Hanon's long reach. His arms swiped at her like chains, each one trying to tear her face and hair. Julia gave in to her fear. She hadn't even hunted a handful of feral vampires and I was more worried for her than I was for myself because I couldn't take care of her. She backed away past me, with Mr. Hanon's arms swirling wildly. I watched her with despair as she went near the window.

"Julia! Look out!" I cried. Panic lined her face as she came to the open window. The air seemed to tug at her, and the only way she could get out of Mr. Hanon's reach was to fall back. She screamed and I was about to run to her when Mrs. Thorpe grabbed me back. Mr. Hanon leaped out of the window and there was nothing more I could do for Julia. I turned around and slammed my elbow down onto Mrs. Thorpe's arm. The bone cracked and her limb dangled unnaturally from the elbow. She hissed and nipped at me with her jaws. I twisted back and put my hands on the table, spinning my legs around, where I kicked her in the face using all the momentum of my body. I spun back and landed on my feet, jabbing the stake down in one fluid movement, but I missed her heart as she twisted away, writhing in pain. There was no time to waste. I had to defeat them soon, because the longer they stayed alive the more chance there was that they would defeat me. There were so many ways for them to hurt me, and I'd always been told that a Slayer being turned into a vampire was a very bad thing.

I wasn't going to let that happen to me.

I wasn't going to let it happen to Julia either, although she was on her own for the moment. I heard some muffled screams and some scuffles outside, but I couldn't get to the window. Blood dripped down my wrist and I wiped it on my top. I pulled out another stake and held it in my hand even though the pain throbbed. Mr. Griff was so arrogant he stood there waiting for the inevitable. Mrs. Thorpe cackled and howled as she pushed herself up, her one broken limb dangling limply, the other one clawing her way across the table. I took the measure of her movements and anticipated where she was going to be. I drove one stake through the side of her head and then pushed her onto her back. I drove the stake down into her heart, feeling it split her ribs. I used all my strength to hammer it through her chest and the cackling laughter stopped.

I panted. Sweat dripped down my cheeks.

Mr. Griff applauded slowly.

"You're quite the Slayer aren't you? Some are better than others. I've known a few in my time. She's not the best," he cast a withering glance out of the window towards Julia. I couldn't hear anything from her.

"This ends now," I said. I gripped my stakes tightly and jumped on the table, striding towards him. As I did so he smirked and his hands slammed against the side of the table. I lost my balance and tumbled down, the stakes rolling out of my grip as I tried to steady myself.

"You'll need to be cleverer than that," Mr. Griff said. "It's such a shame the council has corrupted your mind so much. They do tell Slayers the most horrid things about us. You know that they're as bad as us, right? They want to control the world as much as we do, they're just annoyed that there's no way they can make Slayers themselves. They have to wait for the bloodlines to do their work. You might think you're doing some sacred duty, but you're really just another link in the chain, and it seems it's time for this link to be broken."

He opened his mouth and stepped onto the table. He was so tall. I pushed myself up, but he placed his hand on my head and squeezed. His bony fingers dug into my scalp and I felt him placing pressure on my skull. I slapped his arms, but his strength was unmatched and I didn't seem to be able to break his hold on me. I reached out for my stakes, but they were just out of reach and he had such a powerful hold on me I couldn't even move far enough to get them. I strained my fingers, trying to will them towards me, but that didn't work either.

"It's such a shame really that Slayers are so brainwashed, because I think in partnership we could achieve great things together," he said. It didn't even sound as though he was exerting any undue effort to keep me down, and I felt like such a poor Slayer for being in this position. I should have put up more of a fight. I should have been better.

I screamed until my lungs were raw as I tried to break free. I thought for a moment he was going to rip my scalp off. Hot tears streamed down my cheeks as he kept his grip so tight on my head, and then the doors opened.

Josh, Adam, and Troy stood there.

"Ah, my boys," Mr. Griff said. "Sadly your mother has died, but now we can punish this Slayer as a family. You should be proud that you finally get to experience what it's like to prove yourself superior to one of these pests," he said. I looked at the boys with pain in my eyes. Their expressions were vacant and I had no idea if I could trust them or not. I know I had betrayed Josh when I told him that I was a Slayer. I had killed one of the vampires who had given them life. I was sure that Julia had already died, and I was soon to follow. The bloodline ended with me. I hadn't done enough to secure my legacy. All of my ancestors had been wasted because I couldn't keep the chain going.

The only boys I had given my heart to were vampires, and now they were going to kill me unless I managed to do something drastic.

"Please, Josh," I groaned, reaching out towards him, "help me. He...he's hurting me. I'm sorry. I didn't want this. All I want is you. Help me..."

It was an attempt to break the control that their masters had on them. I wasn't sure that it would work. If I had more time I might be able to make a difference, but Mr. Griff and the others had given them life. What had I done that was comparable?

I had to close my eyes because I was in so much pain and I didn't want to put myself through the anguish of having to watch them obey their masters.

"How pitiful it is to hear you plead," Mr. Griff sneered. "Slayers always have this superior attitude to them and it's nice to see you being put in your place. Sadly you won't get to learn from your mistake because there's not going to be a chance for you to learn anything anymore. You're going to be nothing more than a test for my boys here. I did find it quite amusing that you would think you could influence them. I can't really blame them I suppose. Boys will be boys, and they certainly showed good instincts in choosing a Slayer. Now then, I think it's quite poetic to kill this Slayer with her own weapon. Which one of you would like to oblige?" he said, each word dripped with malicious intent and I continued to wince. The pain in my scalp felt as though a thousand tiny needles were prickling against my skin. I shook my head, trying to warn them off.

"No...no..." I gasped.

"I'll do it," Josh said. Of course it had to be Josh. He walked forward and I forced myself to open my eyes to look at him. He looked so different when compared to just a short time ago on the bench. He must have come straight back here, gathered Adam and Troy, and told them what was happening. They were in thrall to these masters and their place was at the Academy. I should have sensed this sooner. My downfall was my own fault. I had nobody to blame but myself and I only wished that I had been kinder to Arthur. If I had listened to him more I might have been better prepared for this.

I watched Josh reach over and pick up the stake. He licked his lips as he held the weapon of the Slayer in his hand. My throat ran dry and at this point I was just glad that the moment was soon going to be over. Maybe the Slayers were a dying race and vampires were the future. Maybe I was just a failure at this, just as I had been a failure at everything, but I would never get to have a family of my own. I would never know what it was like to fall in love. I would never get to make my parents proud.

"I'm sorry..." I whispered. It was an apology to my parents, to Arthur, to my ancestors, and to myself. Josh leaned over the table. He stood beside his master.

"I'm proud of you Josh," Mr. Griff said.

I looked up at Josh and wished I knew what to say. I wanted to tell him that I only ever wanted to be close to him. My fondest memory of life had been with the three of them under the moonlight. That was going to be my last thought. I closed my eyes and remembered how good I felt being so intimate and close with them, and then I surrendered to the inevitable, waiting for the feeling of my heart being punctured.

# Chapter Sixteen

I was all ready to embrace the sweet pain and tumble down into oblivion, to finally be freed from the shackles of life. I thought about what Adam had said to me and how there was some beauty in death. I tried to think of that, even though I felt I was too young for that and hadn't accomplished everything I wanted in life. In the end I was just like my parents, dying before their time, but at least they had been together when it all ended. I was by myself and everything ended with me.

But the final moment didn't come. My skin was not pierced by the stake, and I didn't feel the pain of life slipping away. I heard a grunt from Mr. Griff and opened my eyes. Josh had driven the stake into Mr. Griff's heart unexpectedly. The headmaster's face was a picture of shock before his body crumbled into dust, leaving behind nothing but a faint odor and the lingering presence of evil.

Josh still had the stake in his hand and I was scared. But then he dropped it and he ran to me. They all did. I was surrounded by Adam, Troy, and Josh. They smiled and I breathed with relief. I wrapped my arms around the three of them, holding them close.

"What happened?" I asked.

"I thought about what you said," Josh replied. "When I came back I talked about it with Adam and Troy. We all agreed that it was about time we decided things for ourselves. We didn't like what they wanted for our future, and we didn't like being at the mercy of their whims. With you we truly felt alive again. It wasn't something we ever thought we'd feel again, and we knew we couldn't let you die. This was the way it had to be, and now we pledge ourselves to you."

They bowed their heads, and it brought to mind the dream I had of my ancestor. I realized this wasn't the first time a Slayer had formed a harem of male vampires, but it had been hidden away. The truth was in my mind though, and now it was in front of me. I had been taught that these were creatures of evil, but to me they were instruments of pleasure, they were my boys, my vampires, my lovers. A solemn feeling overwhelmed me as I took them into my arms, taking them from the grip of their masters, and I knew I was going to treat them better.

"We didn't want any part of what they were offering. They expected us to take their place and to turn others," Adam said.

"I know, I know. Everything is alright now," I cooed.

"We only fed on animals because we have to," Troy said. "I tried to have fun, but they were so serious. They kept holding the fact that they had saved our lives over our heads. All I wanted was to move on from cancer, but they never let us forget it."

"You can forget about it now. This is a new beginning. We're going to create new traditions and you don't have to worry about a thing. I'm going to take care of you," I said, although I was making promises I wasn't sure I would be able to keep. This relationship went against all my training and I knew the council wouldn't be happy. Neither would Arthur. But this felt right and as I looked at them I knew I didn't want anything else, or anyone. I knew that nothing else was going to make me happy. The fact that they were vampires and I was a Slayer seemed secondary. All that mattered was that we were together.

"What's going to happen now?" Troy asked, looking at the dust that had settled over the tables, chairs, and floor. I didn't know how this was going to be explained away. I assumed the council would cover it up somehow, they always did. But there was something else. I turned around.

"Julia!" I called.

"She's alright. We saved her as we were coming to you. We told her to be quiet," Adam said.

"Can I come out now?" Julia asked. She pulled herself through the window and dusted herself off, and then she looked at me and the three men. Her eyes gleamed with hunger and she held her stake tightly. "Get away from them Elsa," she said.

I stepped forward protectively, spreading my arms.

"You know our deal Julia. I told you that these are to be left unharmed," I said.

"They're vampires. They have to be dealt with," she said.

"They're not. They're under my protection and I don't care what you or anyone else says. These aren't evil vampires. We've been looking at this all wrong. They're not posing any threat to anyone, so let's just leave things where they are and get back to Arthur."

"I can't do that Elsa. Arthur and I had a little chat when you were getting ready. He was worried that something like this might happen, and he gave me direct instructions to deal with you if you became too much trouble. You're a Slayer. You're supposed to kill vampires, not fuck them. You've betrayed us Elsa, and now you're going to pay the price."

I knew there wasn't going to be any way to reason with her, or talk her down. I had saved her life before, but now she was out for my blood. I wasn't even angry with her. I was angry with Arthur for giving her those orders. He should have spoken to me, should have trusted me. I couldn't believe that he would go behind my back like this, but then when I thought about it how much did I really know him? Some of the council's practices had always seemed shady and they were very rigid in their traditions. I guess I wasn't meant to be a Slayer after all.

"You know I'm going to beat you Julia," I said.

"We'll see. I've been watching you closely Elsa. I've learned your moves. I'm not going to be a pushover. I'm better than some feral vampire."

I was already tired from the battle. My wrist ached and my scalp throbbed. I stepped forward though, determined to protect my boys. They offered to fight for me, but I told them not to. This was my fight. Besides, for all of Julia's inexperience she was still a Slayer and still equipped with weapons that were deadly to them.

*

Julia had a look of relish on her face as we came together in the middle of the room, away from the table. We held our stakes, and circled each other, taking the measure of us.

"Arthur said you were one of the most naturally gifted Slayers he's ever seen, but I'm going to prove him wrong now. My Mom was one of the best, and I'm going to prove that I'm even better," Julia said. I remained silent, keeping my breath even and making sure to observe her movements carefully. I watched the way she stepped, and how far she reached. I let her speak, hoping that it would distract her. When I saw an opening I surged forward and lowered my body, crashing into her legs. She yelped and fell back, steadying herself against a chair. Her hair cascaded down her face in thin strands and her eyes were dark and glowering. She shrieked as she came towards me, arms flailing about. Her attacks were fierce and deadly, but they were also wild and inaccurate. I managed to evade them all and fought back with a jab of my own in her gut. I twisted around and elbowed her in her back, right where her kidneys were located. I hadn't used my stake yet. I didn't want to kill her, all I wanted was for her to stop fighting me.

"Give it up Julia. You can walk away from this. I just want to be left alone," I said.

"Never! I'm going to prove myself the best damn Slayer there ever was. My Mom died for this!" she cried, and came at me again, screaming loudly, thrusting her stake through the air, trying to stab me. I dodged quickly and her blows narrowly missed. I could tell she wasn't going to stop unless I made her stop. I gritted my teeth and clenched my jaw. I wasn't just fighting for myself now, I was fighting for my boys as well. Julia had been a thorn in my side ever since we met and I wasn't about to let her have the final word. She came at me and I parried her blow. She was out to kill, wielding her stake like a knife. I countered her moves and stepped back, leading her forward, waiting for the opportunity I needed to strike.

I was supposed to be a vampire Slayer, not a killer of humans. However, I wondered if there was really much difference? Ever since I had become aware of this world I had thought of vampires as nothing but monstrous creatures, but now it was clear that some of them at least were kind and still had souls, while some humans were cold and callous. There had been moments when I thought there was hope for Julia and that she might actually find a way through her pain towards the light, that she would change her way of thinking and become a better person. When she became a Slayer I thought that she would see her potential and that the new perspective of the world would help her realize that there was more to life than being vindictive and spiteful. Instead, it had made her crazed with power. I felt even worse knowing that Arthur had obviously given her this directive. His betrayal came from the heart, her betrayal was just her being a bitch.

I never intended to kill her. I never wanted to cause that much harm to another person, but as she came at me I knew I wasn't going to have a choice. There was only so much defensive work I could do to deflect her blows. At some point I had to strike back. She screamed like a banshee and I continued backing away, waiting for the right moment. I watched her hands flail about and then, when the time was right, I shifted my weight onto my back foot and angled my body back, kicking her in the middle of the chest. I struck with such impact that she was thrust back as though she had been hit by a car. Her body crumpled and cracked as it slammed against the rear wall, and her head jerked. There was a sickening crack as her body slumped to the ground, and the stake rolled out of her hand, sliding limply against the table. Her head lolled to the side and her eyes were lifeless. It had happened instantly and I rushed to her, hoping that there was still some flicker of life inside her, but there wasn't.

I hung my head. This day had extracted a heavy toll, and it shouldn't have been that way. I was supposed to save people, not kill them, but with Julia I had no choice.

# Chapter Seventeen

The boys came around me to support me.

"It wasn't your fault," Josh said.

"She attacked you. She had it coming," Troy added. Adam remained silent. I stared at Julia's lifeless body and then looked around at the dust that had settled on the table and chairs; the only remnants of the master vampires. I bowed my head in sorrow for Julia, and then turned to face the men I loved, the men who had saved me.

"Thank you," I said. Troy took my hand and squeezed it gently. I looked at each of them in turn and offered them appreciative smiles. I rested my head against Josh's strong body, and I breathed out in a long exhalation. My body trembled after all the strain, and the pain still throbbed from where I had been wounded.

"Why did she attack you like that?" Adam asked.

"Because she was ordered to, by my watcher. Slayers aren't supposed to fraternize with vampires like we do. She was told to take care of me if I showed any sign of disloyalty. They weren't going to let me get away with my feelings for you," I said.

"But you did anyway?" Josh asked.

"Of course. I'm not going to obey anything that tells me these feelings are wrong. Being with you is the only thing that's ever felt right to me. I'm just sorry that Julia had to pay the price, although she never had the mentality to be a true Slayer. She was always too hot-headed. Arthur made a mistake in sending her with me...I will have to have words with him," I said with grim determination. My face turned to stone. Everything I knew was crumbling before me. The academy had turned out to be a sham, my mentor had sent someone to kill me behind my back, and I had killed a fellow Slayer. I wasn't sure what the punishment for that was, but I knew it wouldn't be a good one.

"Why did you come for me? I thought you weren't going to leave your masters?" I asked.

Josh glanced at the other two. "After you left me I was afraid and angry. I couldn't believe that you were a Slayer, or that I had fallen in love with you. But then I thought about what you said, about if we were really free. I thought about a lot of things actually. You know I've always been thinking about what happens to our soul-"

"Josh, if there's one thing I'm sure of it's that you have more soul than Julia ever did. I'm starting to think that everything I was taught about vampires was wrong. I don't think you're soulless, and I don't think you have to be worried about being anything less than you are...any of you," I said, hoping to reassure them.

"Thank you Julia. That's what I've been thinking about. On the way home I thought about the kind of man I wanted to be and I realized that undeath didn't have to be the end of things. We have been given a second chance at life which very few people get, and we were wasting it. And I thought that if I was able to still dream and hope for things, if I was still able to fall in love, then maybe I did have a soul after all. And it's such an elusive and ethereal thing there's no definitive answer anyway. There's nobody who can turn around and tell me that I don't have a soul."

"Exactly. The same holds true for all of you, and I don't think I could have fallen in love with any of you if you didn't have souls. If there wasn't something special and unique about you then I think you would all be the same, and that wouldn't be very fun at all," I said. Given the overwhelming nature of the situation it was easy for me to fall into my emotion and focus on my love for them. I was drained and exhausted, and the adrenaline was still rushing through my system. The shock of it all meant that I hadn't processed the finality of Julia's death even though her dead body was sitting near us. I also wasn't ready to think about the betrayal I had suffered. It niggled at the back of my mind, as though it was trying to remind me of something, but I couldn't face it yet. I wanted to focus on the warmth of intimacy and affection.

"Adam, from the moment we met I was intrigued by your quiet nature. You seemed removed from the world, but I had a feeling you had something interesting to say. In botany class we spoke and I was struck by your affection for the plants. Your profound interest and way of looking at the world really struck a chord with me, and when we kissed it was special. I know you might not have realized how special it was at the time, but I wanted to be close to you." As I said this I noticed Josh and Troy arch their eyebrows. Neither Adam nor I had made mention of the fact that we had kissed in the midnight gardens, but no comment was made.

"I know that you have suffered sorrow in your life and you have been hard on yourself," I continued, "but that is no reason to stop yourself from feeling the kind of love that you deserve. I learned a long time ago that you can't force anyone to feel anything. I used to try my hardest with the people who came around the orphanage. I always wished that they would love me, but for one reason or another they never chose me and that didn't make me any less of a person. It didn't make me any less worthy of love, just like your experience hasn't made you any less worthy. You're such a compassionate and kind-hearted person. I know you only want the best for the world and the best for me, and I'm grateful for that. I promise that I will always take care of you and I trust that you will never hurt me, just like I shall never hurt you. We will all look after each other and it's going to be wonderful."

I turned to Troy. "Troy," I said, with a smile on my face, "you have always been so enthusiastic and eager to try new things. I have never gotten the sense that you are burdened by anything. You try your best at life and you always strive to push yourself, whether it's on the basketball court or in your personal life. I wish I hadn't been forced to see Mrs. Thorpe because I would have loved to have seen you play, and I'm sure I'll get the opportunity at some point. You're strong, confident, and enthusiastic. I know that you'll help to push and encourage each of us to be better versions of ourselves."

Then I turned to Josh. I took his hand and squeezed it happily. Although Adam had been the first one of the three I had kissed, Josh was the first one I had fallen for. I smiled widely at him and there was an unspoken sentiment that passed between us, as though we understood that we would always be there for each other no matter what.

"Josh, Josh, Josh," I said, "what can I say about you? You were the first one I met. You were the first friendly face I saw around here. I don't think I would have survived that first day had I not enjoyed that conversation with you, as it proved that I could make friends and that there were some nice people in the academy. I wanted to try and get to know you, but there always seemed to be something you were holding back. Now I know what it was. You tried to explain yourself to me and you've always been struggling with your identity. But I think we all know that you are your own man. You're going to help us think about our place in the world and always ensure that we're doing the best thing for us."

I stood up and opened my arms, embracing the three vampires.

"You three are the most wonderful men I've ever known, and I'm not going to let any harm come to you. Your previous masters neglected you and forced you into this life. I'm going to make sure that you become the best people you can be. We're going to escape this academy and go somewhere else. We're going to start a new life where we can be free of all of this."

"Where are we going? And what will happen to this place? Should we clean anything up?" Josh asked.

"The council of watchers know exactly what has been going on here. Arthur will have told them. They'll be by soon to clean up the mess, and they won't let the truth come out. They can't afford to let the world know that vampires exist, or that a Slayer has been killed. But we should leave before anyone else comes in," I said. We dragged Julia's body behind the table and locked the office behind us so that it wouldn't be easily found. We scurried back through the darkness towards the dorms. Thankfully the academy was so big that sound didn't carry too far and the commotion we caused hadn't roused anyone. It also helped that the masters had been secretive and wouldn't allow anyone near their office either.

I tried not to think about the future of this place because it was doomed. I wasn't sure what my future held either. I had to confront Arthur and perhaps my entire role as a Slayer was in jeopardy, but somehow that didn't seem important any longer. With the vampires flanking me I knew I had everything I needed and I wasn't going to let anything else bring me down.

*

We entered Josh's dorm. The hallways were quiet as everyone else was sleeping. I led the three of them and opened the curtains a crack so I could look up at the moon.

"Beautiful, isn't she?" Josh said. The boys came around me. Josh stood behind me and I felt his arms curling around my waist. I smiled and leaned back, resting my head against his body. I patted his arm and felt the soft hair that stopped at his wrist. I felt underneath his wrist and to my surprise there was a pulse.

"How are you doing that?" I asked.

"I guess there are some things even Slayers don't know," Josh teased. "You want to tell her Troy?"

"Sure, basically whenever we feed it brings us closer to what you'd class as human, which is how the experienced vampires are able to blend into the human world so easily. As long as we keep feeding we can have a pulse and blood flows through our body," Troy said.

"I suppose that explains something else," I said, pressing my hips against Josh's body, grinding myself against him. I smiled when I felt a twitch. "But I think if I want a lesson in vampire anatomy I should have a hands on lesson," I said. I turned around and kissed Josh passionately. With my hands I reached over and brought Troy and Adam in to me as well. I moved from Josh to kiss the others, and held them all tightly. I wished I could express my love for them even more deeply than was possible physically. I wanted to show them how much they meant to me, and I'm sure that they felt the same. I had broken the loyalty they had to their masters. Their devotion to the people who had saved them from death wasn't as much as their devotion for me. I was their new mistress, their new salvation, and I would treat them better than any vampire ever could. I was a Slayer, and even though my destiny was supposed to be to kill vampires, I knew now that I could do nothing but love these ones.

"Get on the bed," I said. They turned around and marched to the double bed. It looked like it was going to be far too small for all of us, but I didn't care about that because it just meant that we were going to have to get close and personal. They sat on the bed, looking up obediently at me, and the memory of the dream flashed back in my mind. I remember the surge of arousal that came with the image of the three vampires kneeling before me. I had their trust, their devotion, and their obedience. I looked down at them and bestowed my blessing upon them. The pain and anguish from the battle had been replaced with something far more frantic and frenetic.

I pulled off their clothes. One by one they became naked, their flesh exposed to me. I ran my fingers along their necks and shoulders, down the middle of their chests. I pushed them down so that they were flat on their backs and then I undressed them completely. I pulled away their pants, tugging them down before flinging them to the floor. I tossed their underwear away. There was no shame among any of them. Their erections were on display for me, standing tall and strong. Vampiric blood surged through them and I felt drool seeping out of the corners of my mouth.

"Don't move," I cooed gently. I plied their flesh with my hands, tracing lines all over their bodies. Adam's was the thinnest, but there was beauty in the way the skin clung to his bones. Josh was the hairiest, and my hands felt nice as they ran through the tangle of hair that sprouted from his chest. Troy was in the best shape. His muscles rippled and his skin was taut under my hands. Each one of them had their own unique beauty and delights. It was a feast of flesh and it was all for me. I teased them by dragging my fingers lightly down the middle of their bodies, making them shudder and tingle.

I shuddered and tingled myself.

I curled my legs underneath my body and sighed as I leaned over to play with each of them. I had two hands and a mouth, and I made good use of them. I used them as a bed to rest my body and idly played and toyed with their erections. I felt the taut skin and ran my nails along the rippling veins. I kissed each of them lightly with my mouth, and took great delight in hearing the soft rush of breath that erupted from their lips as I bestowed pleasure upon them.

I breathed in their masculine scents and dragged my tongue up down their bodies, leaving a trail of saliva behind me. I buried myself in them, and the arousal grew within me. I felt a deep throbbing inside me, an ache that originated deep within my soul, but soon spread out to reach the tips of my toes and fingers. I wanted to drown in their flesh.

After playing with them, teasing them with strokes and squeezes and playful tickles to their smooth tips, I twisted away from their impressive symbols of lust and fell back, draping myself upon the three of them.

"Place your hands upon me," I said. Immediately their hands fell on my body and began groping me. I laughed with delight. It was a deep, throaty laugh and it echoed through the quiet atmosphere in the room. I was fully ready to let myself go and embrace these dark desires. Their fingers crawled over me, eager to explore and slip underneath my clothes to get to me. Their touch was erotic and sensual. I closed my eyes, again loving the mystery of not knowing whose hand was touching me where. One of them had his hand resting on my throat, curling slightly, placing just enough pressure to keep it exciting.

Another's hand slipped under my top and his finger circled my nipple. It hardened instantly. Breath rushed out of me as I arched my body and felt the finger run around the nipple, moving up and down and around, eliciting a great deal of pleasure from me. My skin felt as though it was on fire. Nails dug into the soft flesh of my breasts and I groaned with delight. My nipples were so sensitive and it felt wondrous to be touched there.

Then I twitched and writhed as another hand traveled down my thigh, squeezing tightly, the fingers searching to get ever closer, teasing and tempting, and it was at this point that I realized I had far too many clothes on. Sweat prickled all over my body and I was uncomfortably warm. I yearned for them. I was so hungry I wanted to feel their flesh against mine, to lose myself in this sea of undulating flesh once again. The intimacy under the moon in the gardens had been but a taster. This time I wanted to go all the way, to live up to my ancestor and embrace everything these vampires had to offer.

I got them to support me as I rose and then they undressed me. I could feel the desire in their bodies as they peeled away my clothes. We enjoyed deep kisses as they took my garments away and left me naked. They gazed at me in awe and they all asked permission to touch.

"Ravish me," I said and fell back on the bed as the three vampires came over me like hungry beasts. Their hands and lips were all over me, leaving thunderous hot kisses over my skin. They nibbled and bit and I laughed gloriously again. Adam suckled on my breasts while Troy kissed my mouth, and I groaned as Josh buried himself in between my thighs. He lifted one leg of mine and hooked it around his neck before he started lapping at me with his eager tongue. I saw his mound of hair sliding up and down as he made love to me with his mouth, and I felt his tongue dancing inside me. The pleasure was electric and overwhelming. For a moment I thought it was going to be too intense for me and that I was going to pass out, but the pleasure never threatened to stop and I wasn't going to end it.

Their bodies were heavy against mine and I was almost crushed by their weight. I wrapped my arms around them and held them tightly as our mouths mingled. At one point the vampires shifted position and changed what they were doing. I was so lost in the whirlpool of my own mind that I had no idea it had happened until I looked down and they were all in different positions. I reached out and grabbed the nearest erection I could find, wanting to feel their lust. My mouth opened in hunger and low, guttural moans burst out.

I dug my nails into their skin and heard them wince. I watched them give themselves to me. I pulled Troy closer and smeared the warmth of his erection over my mouth, feeling the heat spread from my cheeks to my forehead. I opened my mouth and sucked eagerly, wanting to reward him and thank him for coming to my aid. I swirled my tongue around his thick shaft and heard him moan. Occasionally my mouth hung open because the pleasure I received from Adam going down on me was too much. Josh was at my breasts now and our hands linked together in one long, endless chain. My soul broke open and hot molten lust poured out.

I gagged on Troy's cock and left it dripping with saliva. I was hungry for more and then I let out a huge moan as Adam hoisted up my legs and made my body arch completely. I shrieked with delight and the pleasure increased, not that I thought that was even possible. Troy's erection escaped me and my head crashed against the pillow. The rush of exhilaration gave me a titillating delight and orgasmic energy swelled and spread through me. It rushed through me like a juggernaut, taking every breath I had with it. My body shuddered and trembled. The inferno seized me and my eyes clamped shut as my mind cracked and everything poured out. I screamed so hard I thought I would wake up the whole academy, the whole city, and my body rocked with an intense burst of pleasure.

My eyes widened and I gasped with shock at the strength. I had no idea what it would have been on the Richter scale but it felt off the charts to me. I smiled and whimpered and knew I needed more. Oh God, where was this deep ache coming from? How could I be this much of a slut? It felt as though I was making up for all the years of dormancy and loneliness. I craved for more. I needed it all. Tears welled up in my eyes, such was the intensity of my desire, and I looked to my vampires.

"Fuck me," I said, my weak and trembling voice laced with desperation and urgency. "I need you. I need more. God, fuck me, fuck my brains out!" I yelled. Josh, Adam, and Troy looked at each other.

"Which one," they asked. My head twisted from side to side. I felt the errant hair falling all over my face.

"I don't care," I groaned, "all of you. I want all of you. One after the other."

I spread my legs and saw my pussy and thighs glisten with sweet wetness. The warm liquid seeped down my legs and as the moonlight that poured in through the window caught it, it seemed to come to life and shimmer, as though it was magical and enchanted. It certainly felt that way.

I couldn't quite believe that I had gone my entire life without experiencing anything like this. I had always wondered why people had been obsessed with sex. I never assumed it could be this good, but damn, my body thrummed and quivered. I didn't think I would ever walk the same again and I had only had one orgasm. I felt for sure that I was going to explode, with everything that was bubbling and simmering inside me. I had never felt more alive than I had in that moment. Everything else paled in comparison to these sensations. Nothing else mattered, and I had a feeling that I wouldn't be able to feel these things with anyone other than these vampires.

The energy that swirled and surged within me felt as though it had taken on a life of its own. It was as though I was at the mercy of this entirely new organism and it wasn't going to let me sleep or rest until it had been fully satisfied. My vision became blurred. The vampires were nothing more than vague figures before me. I felt one of them grab my thighs and suddenly he was inside me, stretching my tight Slayer pussy. My head lolled back and my hands gripped the bed sheets as I felt him getting deeper and deeper inside me. My legs were spread and he pounded away, thrusting hard. My hair fell over my mouth as my rampant breaths went in and out. My skin sizzled and sweat pooled in the valley of my breasts. I felt hands groping my nipples and then suddenly there was a finger in my mouth. I sucked hard. It seemed the natural thing to do. I heard guttural grunts and moans, the sounds of masculine intensity. The hammering rhythm increased as did the ache between my thighs, and then all of a sudden there was sweet relief and bliss. Warmth spread through me with a jerk of the hips and a smile spread across my face.

My mind crackled with electricity and it was hazy and delirious. I had basically lost my sense of time and space. The moment I shared with them seemed to be everlasting and I wasn't ready to leave that bed. I had a feeling it would last forever. The ecstasy of the orgasm was such that it rendered me unable to think about anything else. I whimpered as I felt my body being lifted and twisted. I scrambled to be on all fours, and then I felt a few fingers playing with my soaking wet pussy before a huge erection entered me from behind. I felt hands running down my spine, resting on my rump, reaching around and groping my breasts. I was being made love to by a stallion and the strong, steady rhythm started again. He was steadier than before, stronger and deeper too. I imagined it must have been Troy. He squeezed my hips and I felt his strength. I felt him get deep inside me, deeper than I ever thought possible. He was so deep I thought for a moment he was going to tear me apart, but that only added to the excitement. He was primal and savage. I felt the passion in every inch of his erection and I loved the feeling of my body being pounded from behind, ramming me with every ounce of his might. I felt completely at his mercy and I was driven to a state of near insanity with every thrust of his body.

When his orgasm hit him, he built up to it by getting faster and faster. He held onto me tightly and grabbed a fistful of my hair, and then he rumbled and thundered and came like a volcano. I felt it trickle down my thighs. I was such a mess, but I didn't care, I was still hungry. I wanted more. I finally knew what it was like to be a vampire, to have this incessant, unending hunger that needed to be fed, else it would drive you insane.

I twisted around and groggily found Josh. I placed my hands on his shoulder and pushed him back so that he lay flat on the bed. I climbed onto him and sank down onto his cock, the feeling of him inside me was just perfect. I pulled my hair from around my face and reared back, letting his hands roam all around my body as I rocked back and forth, controlling the motion and the rhythm. I twisted and grinded, and it felt so damned good. Troy and Adam came beside me. Their fingers ran through my hair and their lips found my gaping mouth. Their hands groped my breasts and as I made love to Josh it felt as though I was making love to all of them. I loved feeling their long, strong arms around me and their breaths washing over my skin. I looked at each of them as I made love and the orgasm that hit me was the strongest one yet. I flung myself forward and made out with Josh, kissing him deeply as the pleasure swam through my body and left me a writhing, whimpering, wrecked mess.

*

I carefully peeled myself off Josh and lay on the bed, my arms splayed out and my chest heaving. My body was slick with sweat and utterly ruined, but I was deliriously happy. Adam rose and came back with a wash cloth. He cooled me down and wiped the sweat from me, caressing me lovingly. I welcomed them all to me and we shared our love and affection. We were all moved by the intensity of the sensations and it was going to take me the entire night to recover. I lost myself in their arms and their love. I didn't care that they were vampires and

I was a Slayer. I didn't care that we weren't supposed to have this love. It felt right. It felt perfect. I wasn't going to let anyone else tell me this was wrong. These were my vampires, and I was going to fight whoever I needed to because what we had was worth fighting for. In fact, I thought, I was going to tell the truth because it was unfair that any Slayer should miss out on an opportunity like this. Not all vampires were our enemies.

It was time for the rules to change.

# Chapter Eighteen

We lay together, the four of us, completely satisfied and fulfilled. A dull ache throbbed through my body, making me feel utterly content and serene. My mind was quiet and I knew that in this moment there was nothing to worry about. Their bodies were pressed against mine and as I looked down at them I felt lucky, and honored, and proud to have the three of them devoted to me. Their loyalty and adoration were precious to me, and I vowed to never let them think they had made a mistake in offering themselves to me. I don't know exactly what I had done to win them over, but I had done enough and they had chosen me over their masters. I had given them love and now I was going to give them a life they were worthy of. I had been left breathless by all the relentless orgasms, but I wasn't ready to think about the future yet. I didn't want to worry about anything. I had no idea what I was going to tell Arthur or how the Council would react. I wasn't sure anything like this had happened before, but I was going to protect my vampires no matter what. Nothing was going to stop us from being together.

Nothing.

I listened to their breathing and the rigors of the day lulled me to sleep. I enjoyed feeling the soft twitches of their hands and arms, and the rhythm of their breaths. I sank into warm slumber, knowing that the day to come was going to be an important one. But the night would not be as restful as I hoped, for a dream came to me, and one final message that would cast everything in a new light.

*

Panic filled me. I was terrified. I scrambled around on the ground, my hands searching for anything that might help me. I looked down and saw the crimson blood bloom across my stomach. My reflection caught on the mirror. I knew I was in my Aunt's final moments again. I writhed and twisted. I tried to scream, but I was filled with horror. The metallic taste of blood swam on my tongue and it choked me. I trembled as I sank to the ground, the strength seeping away from my limbs. My head was woozy and that strange feeling passed through me once again...that feeling of betrayal

She looked up, and I looked through her eyes. I felt the stake in my stomach, but that didn't seem to matter anymore. I saw the figure walking away. I strained to see who it was. There was something familiar about his gait, but I couldn't place it, so distracted was I by the pain, and the anguish, and the feeling of death sweeping in, ready to claim my Aunt.

Then he stopped and looked back.

Now I knew why my Aunt felt betrayed.

"Arthur...I loved you..." she whispered, barely able to get the words out without choking. He turned around. I could barely believe it. It was Arthur. He had blood on his hands. There was pain written on his face.

"I loved you too, but I had to do my duty. I'm sorry. The war comes above everything," he said. That was the last thing she remembered. The world went black, and the last thing she saw was Arthur walking away from her.

*

I awoke and pushed myself bolt upright. The night had been long and now the dawn sun was spreading through the windows. I moved from the bed and drew the curtains so the light wouldn't threaten my vampires. They stirred, and Troy spoke to me.

"Where are you going?" he asked.

"I have to go and see my watcher, explain what happened. I have to tell him this myself. I'll be back soon. I promise." I walked over to them and gave them each a kiss in turn. They offered to come with me, but I told them it was morning. Besides, I didn't want them getting mixed up in this. There was going to be a lot of trouble and I wanted to keep them out of it for as long as possible.

My mind throbbed with pain as I thought about what must have happened. I couldn't believe that Arthur had betrayed my aunt like that, but it made sense given how defensive he was. But why? I had to know, and the only way was to confront him.

There was a lot of news to tell him of course, and I wasn't sure he was going to be happy to see me.

*

On the way to his house (I didn't consider it my home any longer) I thought about being secretive and stealthily working my way in, but I didn't see the point. I threw open the front door. Arthur scurried out.

"Surprised to see me? Or did you think Julia was going to come back with my head on a platter," I asked angrily. Arthur held up his hands.

"I was just taking precautions. You mentioned some affinity for vampires that was troubling. I would have done the same for everyone. Now, are you going to tell me what happened? Where is Julia?" he asked, worry entering his voice.

"Where do you think she is? She's no match for me. She attacked me, under your orders, and I defended myself. Are you surprised?"

"I suppose I shouldn't be. And the vampires?"

"We dealt with them. Thanks to the ones you think are a threat. They helped me overthrow their masters. And now they're under my protection."

"Elsa," he said sternly, "you know that's wrong. I can't allow you to carry on like this. It's not safe. You can't trust them, they're vampires."

"Oh, like I can trust you? Like my Aunt trusted you?"

He barely even flinched. He'd always been asking me about my dreams and now I realized it was because of this moment, because he was afraid of what I would learn about him. Now I knew, and I didn't feel anything but contempt.

"Yes, she trusted me, and if she had listened to what I said she would have been fine. But she didn't, and she met a tragic end."

"Tragic? Arthur, you haven't asked me if I've had a dream lately," I said. That had an effect on him. He tensed and blinked at me. His face reddened, and the uncertainty that appeared in his eyes lasted a couple of moments.

"Yes," I said, "I relived her final moments, and they were tragic indeed. Stabbed with her own stake, having to watch the man she loved walk away. Having to watch you walk away. Tell me Arthur, why did you do it? Why did you betray her? I should have known it earlier. I had my suspicions. I should have listened to my instinct, but I told myself that I was being stupid. I said there wasn't any reason why you would have done that and I was just being paranoid for my own good. But I wasn't being paranoid. You killed her, and all this time you've been keeping it hidden from me. Why?"

I thought he was going to passionately defend himself, or attack me. Instead, he collapsed in the nearest chair and put his head in his hands, weeping desperately. His shoulders trembled and the house was filled with his howling. I didn't move from where I was sitting for I didn't want to risk getting so close to him given I'd seen what he had done to my Aunt, but the emotion he showed seemed genuine.

"I didn't want to do it," he heaved. "I loved her like I've never loved anyone before. It wasn't supposed to happen. Watchers and Slayers are supposed to be professional, nothing more, but your Aunt and I...we fell in love. We even talked about adopting you after your parents died, but we both agreed it was too dangerous. We hid our affection from the council, but they still found out, and your Aunt was plagued with these terrible dreams. She knew there was something off, something different, and she wasn't going to stop until she found out. She was like you, tenacious and determined. She found the book. She found the truth."

"The truth that Vampires and Slayers aren't always at each others' throats?"

He nodded.

"We didn't understand it at first, but the more we looked into the past the more we found more instances of lines being blurred between Slayers and Vampires. The rules that we obey are not written into the fabric of the universe like the council would have us believe. There's more grey area, and some vampires are not the evil creatures they seem to be."

"So what happened?"

"Your aunt wanted to take it to the council. She wanted to share it with the world and tell everyone that we were going about this the wrong way. There's a reason why Slayers are kept isolated. If they share their memories they'll all realize that something is different. At the moment the council keep them apart and it's our job to try and tell you that you're just mistaken, but some people keep looking. They can't let go, but we can't let the truth out."

"Why not? Would it be so bad?"

Arthur looked haggard. I'd never seen him so distraught before. All the bad memories were being dredged up. I knew now why he never seemed to sleep, because he was always haunted by the fact that he had killed the woman he loved. It also explained the torn out page. My aunt must have found it herself and taken it to prove to Arthur what she was seeing, but instead of keeping it safe he took it from her and then took her life.

"Don't you understand? If we begin giving vampires rights the whole world will be in chaos. There are only a few good ones, and they don't deserve our time. They're an abomination, and can you imagine what would happen if a vampire mated with a Slayer? No, no, no, we can't allow that to happen at all. We're at war, and we must remain vigilant until the war ends. It would be all too easy to give up, but we must be strong. We had to keep it hidden. The council know what they're doing and they decreed that this was all to be kept secret. Vampires are a scourge on the world and we cannot do anything to encourage their procreation. They're evil. They always have been and they always will be. We all have our jobs to do, even if they're unpleasant sometimes, but we still have to do them because it's our solemn duty."

I got the sense he was echoing what the council had told him to do.

"So you killed her. For the sake of protecting this lie."

"I had to," he croaked. His voice was dry and bitter. "The war comes above everything. We have to fight against evil. We can't allow it to continue. Your Aunt wanted to ruin that. If she had just agreed to stay quiet I wouldn't have had to do what I did, but she couldn't stay there. She couldn't just let things be. I was given my orders, and I carried them out, because that's what a good soldier does. She threatened our wellbeing, threatened the war, and I wish I hadn't because I loved her, but I had to. I had to."

"No," I said definitively, "You didn't. You chose to, because you and your council don't have the imagination to think of other possibilities. You can't imagine that there's some other way out there. You just want power. You're just as bad as the master vampires themselves. All you want is to rule over your little kingdom and anyone who threatens you is out, and what's worse is that I think you really believe you did something noble, that you made some kind of sacrifice. Well, you didn't. You killed an innocent woman whose only crime was to love you, and then you brought me into it as well. I know you were talking to the council about me. What were your plans for me, were you going to kill me as well?"

"I didn't want to," he groaned. "You reminded me so much of your aunt. But when you started having the same dreams I had to let them know. I had to tell them that you were a threat and I was cautious. I was afraid that you'd find out the truth. I knew that if you did you'd never trust me again and there has to be trust between a Slayer and a Watcher. There has to be. To fight evil we had to have trust."

"You ruined all of that because of what you did. You say you wanted to fight evil, but you became evil. You gave in to fear. You did what you knew was wrong because you were too scared to stand up to the council. I pity my Aunt for loving you. You weren't worthy of her."

Arthur looked utterly pathetic. He was a defeated, broken man. All his sins had caught up with him and now there was no escaping the dark reflection that looked back at him in the mirror. He averted his gaze from mine and stared into space. He looked down at his hands, and I wondered if he was remembering his blood-soaked flesh after he'd murdered my Aunt. My hatred wasn't even for him though; it was for the council who decreed these rules and tried to control us. My blood boiled for them, and I would have my revenge.

"What are you going to do now?" he asked. He gulped. I knew he was afraid that I would kill him, but I wasn't going to do that.

"I'm going to go away with my vampires and find this council. I'm going to find other Slayers and tell them the truth. You tried to shackle us and use us as weapons, but we're not weapons. We're living, breathing beings and we have ambitions of our own. I'm going to change this world and I'm going to make sure that my Aunt didn't die in vain. And I'm going to warn them all about their watchers, because any of them could be stabbed in the back at any time. I'm not going to let that happen ever again."

That was the last thing I said to him. I walked out of the door, and as I turned down the street to put this house behind me forever I heard a gunshot that faded into silence.

# Epilogue

As I suspected, the council used their influence to come up with some fake story about there being a financial scandal where the heads of the academy made off with a great deal of money. It was claimed that Mr. Griff, Mrs. Thorpe, and Mr. Hanon had disappeared into thin air with a whole year's worth of tuition fees, and because they couldn't find anyone to pay the sum needed to keep the academy open it was being closed down. All the students were told to leave, which had caused much consternation and panic as nobody really knew if their qualifications were still going to be honored. It was said that Julia died in an accident as well. Most believed that she had committed suicide in the wake of her parent's death. I wasn't about to tell anyone the truth.

It was strange to see the building so vacant, and there were so many questions left. I didn't know how many other vampires there were or which of the academy graduates had been placed there by the vampire masters. The boys hadn't been privy to any of that information either, so the hunt would have to continue.

We met under the cover of darkness. Adam had rescued a plant from the botany lab, and he was dismayed that he wouldn't be able to take care of the gardens.

"We'll find another one for you," Troy reassured him. I looked over at Josh.

"Are you ready to begin the adventure?" I asked. Josh grinned and pointed in a random direction.

"Let's go that way," he said.

We started walking and I was filled with hope. I had no idea where our path was going to lead us, but I didn't think that anything could stand in the way of a Slayer and her vampire harem. We had been through plenty already, but there was more to come. I knew not every Slayer was going to listen to me, and the council was certainly going to be a formidable enemy, but as long as we were together I knew that nothing was going to hurt us. We'd make our way in this world together, as a family, and I was going to live up to the legacy of my ancestors. I didn't care about rules any longer; although I must say that I never had. I was going to have their babies, and if I had a daughter I wasn't going to keep our true nature a secret. She deserved to know that one day she was going to be a Slayer, and she deserved to know exactly what it meant.

I led them into the darkness, into the future, and my heart raced with excitement.

*****

# Don't miss out!

Visit the website below and you can sign up to receive emails whenever Lilly Wilder publishes a new book. There's no charge and no obligation.

https://books2read.com/r/B-A-KAQD-RUBDC

BOOKS 2 READ

Connecting independent readers to independent writers.

# Also by Lilly Wilder

Indebted To The Vampires
Wolf's Nanny
Bearly Familiar
Protected by the Wolves
Academy For Vampires
Bear Protection
Dragon Dreams
Seduced by Dragons
Her Lion Protectors

www.ingramcontent.com/pod-product-compliance
Lightning Source LLC
LaVergne TN
LVHW041031150826
845672LV00001B/273

* 9 7 9 8 2 2 3 8 3 7 0 5 3 *